THE DO-NOTHING BOYS

Tony Nesca

By Tony Nesca

ISBN - 978-1-7752112-1-1

Printed in The United States of America

Published by:

Screamin' Skull Press

Screamingskullpress.net

Screamin' Skull Press

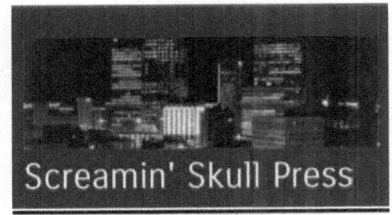

Dedicated to the Fort Garry boys –

What a space in time it was

WHAT YOU ARE ABOUT TO READ IS A WORK OF FICTION

THE DO-NOTHING BOYS

1.

There were ten or twenty or even thirty of us walking down Pembina Highway with open cases of beer getting high and drunk and wandering teenage madness and happiness and tragedy and everything forgotten and parents being nasty and the isolation beautiful and wild...started off just me and my cousin, just the two of us man, me and him wondering laughing sad-happy fuckers,

"Where is everyone tonight?" He said stoned eyes tough and waiting,

"Who fucking cares? I said "Look at how much grass we have"

"Alright man, alright"

But as the night went on we started walking down the main street and people we knew began to fucking pop up,

"Jesus, there's Cindy!" I said

"Baby oh baby"

We waved her over she had a six-pack in hand 16 years old tight jeans rock and roll hair flowing down her shoulders , jean jacket ripped at the elbows, red runners black t-shirt with AC/DC written on it, she came running through traffic, through two boulevards looking all sexy teenage wild,

"I dropped acid about thirty minutes ago" She said

"Alright" Said my cousin

"Max" she said to him "how many times have I told you I loved you?"

"Yeah Max?" I said

"I'm starting to freak out a bit" She said

"No need to freak out with us" I said

Her and my cousin Max kissed opened a beer and we moved into the electric evening...

From there people started joining in without any planning at all, just beautiful random coincidence, one friend after another as the roaming party continued down Pembina Highway past the restaurants and bars and beer vendors and apartment buildings and strip-malls and motels and rock and roll nasty and stopping off at places to score the occasional line of coke and the hell with all the other shit cuz we were fucking young and invulnerable and full of sadness and happy energy and our goddamn parents hated us and we hated them and nothing, absolutely nothing, as beautiful as those hot summer sex-nights and our wild teenage wanderings...

"Ziggy" she says to me,

"Cindy, you beauty luvly, right?"

"You know it"….

We hugged sweet nothings man, sweet delicious moment-by-moment existence and if you listened real closely you could hear the electric guitar in the distance saying BOP BOP FUZZ BOX CRAZY BABY, so 'nother guy from the neighborhood shows up, then another, then some jiggly young girl in my English Lit class, then came the man, Thadeus Nazzie, we called him Nazzie, or The Nazz, or crazy-ass motherfucker, tall and lanky and pill popping good-nature-friend played the drums like a child prodigy father was a cop and a drunk and Nazzie lived hard and fast black leather jacket good guy baby, we all loved The Nazz, had a joint in mouth as he crossed traffic and joined in,

"Let's hit the beer vendor man, I need beer goddamit!" He shouted like the world owed him something and it did,

So we continued down the highway bottles clanging cloud of smoke all around us, a downright moveable feast, a veritable celebration of everything gone wrong, an enormous and absolute beautiful failure dancing down the street with no time left, happy-mojo meanderings with Led Metal in our veins, Max and Cindy arm in arm howling at a world gone dizzy beer bottles raised at the moon, Nazzie moving down the street singing "Highway To Hell" telling strangers he loved them and hated them and wanted them, myself the reluctant leader wilder

than the rest at the head of the bunch leading the boys and girls into battle cuz if you want blood you got it, Judy had finally shown up she my baby doll luvly, my moonlight rock and roll serenade, we were arm in arm kissing and rubbing and gyrating her buxom body in a rhythm all its own luvly and deadly kiss kiss my whistle howling, my temporary madness in time with the cars blowing by in the fucked-up thick heat of the night, there we went lonely-ass horny teenagers with AC/DC and Led Zeppelin and all other things in the urban wild on our minds, HEY HEY PURPLE RAIN MAN, PURPLE ASSHOLE RAIN DAZED AND CONFUSED as I FOUGHT THE LAW AND THE LAW WON…and like I said it ended up about thirty of us cruising that strip like it was ours alone man like Benny Goodman blue the blues on this night and for this night only, where was the large ugly face of authority? Where was the long cool death-hand? What kind of world allowed this teenage rebel- rousing amoral meandering rock and roll sex-drive bikini red fluid down your chin beer-bottle-lonely maryjane looking lean hungry cool desperate kissing wild friends basement party-crazy, what kind of world allowed this mad bad fun-frenzy free-living mind altering boogy-woogy-moondance?

My kind, that's what I say to all you happy-pappy normals out there, my kind baby, and the rock and roll parade continued deeper and deeper into our personal drug-addled madness as we hung out on street corners and smoked cigarettes, drank beer, then continued the life-march hauling ass dizzy with marijuana

and the undying desperation of our teenage lives, we were subnormal, we were outsiders mad bad and dangerous to know, we were all lit up man like bottle rockets in the pitch black night and nothing, nothing could extinguish that impure electricity rolling across the dreary uncaring sky,

"I'm starting to see things man" Said Cindy,

"It's just the acid baby, go with it and whatever you do, don't fight it man" I said,

"What the fuck is that?"

"It's just a cat, don't worry, ("crazy chick" under my breath) it's going to be a blast, ya dig?"

"Alright alright, I dig"

We stopped and suddenly turned back in the direction we came from, reached the end, then went back, two or three times covering the same stretch of highway beer caps strewn all over our trail, the occasional broken bottle, cigarette butts piled high man we smoking till the end of the world and bring it on cuz I ain't worried, we reached a donut place parking lot, paused and looked around....there was a lot of traffic cars pulling in and out, people looking bored and senseless and dead, a tall 6 foot wooden fence at the back, guy came out front door with a white apron on started screaming,

"YOU FUCKING PUNKS AREN'T GOING THROUGH HERE, TURN AROUND AND GET THE FUCK OUT OF HERE"

"We don't want any trouble" I said, everybody paused sensing the wire tighten,

"FUCK OFF YOU STUPID FUCKS!"

That's all I needed, I took off aiming for the fence at the back of the parking lot beer case in hand and took a flying leap grabbing the top of it and bringing it down with me on the other side…fucking nuts baby!…a group of men came running out of the store in our direction and everyone goddamn scrambled, I bolted down the lane followed by Nazzie and Cindy, took a quick look back saw three fucking huge guys on our ass and Max behind them running in the opposite direction with a few other fucks after him, whoa, everyone else blasted off and it was madness at the end of the dung-colored rainbow, it was wildfire running rampant through your brain, it was electric teenage revolution man, "follow me" I said to Nazzie and Cindy who was trippin' by this time but she could really move keeping up without a hitch talking to her the whole time keeping things cool as we zig-gagged through the residential neighborhood hopping fences and bolting through backyards until those lazy-ass morons slowed down, then stopped, then disappeared, and we cooled it and we laughed and we cracked a beer and sat our asses on a curb the crescent moon high up in the black night full of endless laughter…

2.

I lived in my father's basement, fully self-contained suite kitchen washroom living room huge stereo with hundreds of records (courtesy of my brother who had taken off with my mother), parents recently divorced mother back in Italy father working 12 hours a day while my lazy ass cut classes and experimented with sex, drugs, booze and insanity…feeling mighty righteous at that time internally fucked-up over my parent's divorce, outwardly defiant and my powers in full force had almost unlimited energy as was continually pointed out to me, ate very little, drank a lot, used various intoxicants marijuana being the baseline drug underlining the entire affair, we smoked constantly and voraciously and not one of us, NOT ONE displaying the stereotypical "stoner" behavior, none of us were dopes, none of us spoke unintelligently, we had average grades, even failing grades, but when we wanted we passed or did better, we searched far and wide and deep into ourselves and we always hungered man, it was a boogy-woogy-slide-guitar manic swingtown Friday night in the bittersweet high school romance, so there we were last month of school, sometime in June, at the very beginning of the year I had announced I would be failing, "what the fuck for?" said Max, "to make a point" I said, "yeah?... what's that?" "that it's more noble to be a loser than a winner, and that education means shit to me" "good for

you" said Nazzie shaking my hand bloodshot eyes wry grin...but the last month is where we are Monday afternoon teacher at front called Miss Brock she was young and hot long hippie hair, constant mini-skirts, juicy well-sized thighs, she had asked me to purchase some Kiss/Ted Nugent tickets for her and seeing that our whole gang was going I had agreed, she liked our group and I sensed she was one of us, somewhere inside buried underneath the usual bullshit societal necessities she was one of us, we worked quietly on an English report as she slowly walked around the room in and out of the rows of desks her thighs passing me time and time again and my teenage cock as hard as it gets crossing my legs and pretending to write my eyes darting from side to side what an amazing memory, what an incredible moment of uncensored beauty, she sat on the front of her desk facing the class those big tanned legs spreading out on the wood and her painted toes dangling over the edge encased in brown hippie sandals, whoa, our eyes met for an instant, she winked going back to her book and crossed her legs, hmmmmm, Shannon Anderson sat at the front considered widely, along with her best friend Donna Simms, to be the hottest chick in school, our whole gang had hung out the previous year with Shannon, Donna and their friends, but an incident happened with the jocks of the neighborhood involving those girls and us, and they were replaced by an entirely different group of rock and roll chicks, but we never forgot, we still dug each other talking and laughing Donna glancing over as we passed in the

hall remembering that night we made out like demons after a heavy hash session, me and her on the couch right in the middle of the party, then on the floor, then in the bedroom lights off feeling each other up over our jeans, but that was over like all things eventually so no need for remorse and sadness but the sadness she singing anyway, she singing and crying and hollering the midnight blues of loss and unrequited love and teenage desperation…

Class over out in the hall everyone screaming and laughing and feeling destructive cuz internally we were in the throes of the deep wonder-sad blues and he was there all of a sudden, right there all 6'3" of him towering over the entire situation with his burnout cool, jean jacket, long hair man lanky and easy-joe-lovely,

"Ross you hound dog" I said,

"Zigg, you're an asshole…let's go…" He shows me a bomber inside his jacket, big fucking smile then leads the way to the doors past the other hopeless wonderstruck little shits that would amount to sweet-fuck-all in the grim daylight reality, out we go blasting into the beautiful sin-light make for the back fence and huddle sparking reefer and inhaling deep,

"When's your next class?" Said Ross,

"Right away" I said blowing out smoke,

"Crazy fucker, you're going to be blasted!" he laughed,

"Fuck'em" I laughed,

"See ya here, right after class?"

"Yeah, where we going?"

"Down to the park, got lots of beer, ripped it off from the old man"

"Good stuff"

"Heard that new Clash record?"

"London Calling? It's fucking amazing.."

"Alright, you fuck" said Ross "you'd better get to class"

"Yeah, like you care, alright baby, see ya later"

Class was bullshit, nothing else…

So there we were at our usual meeting place, the 7-11 on the corner of Pembina and Crane in a working class neighborhood called Fort Garry, me and Ross and a 24 of beer smoking cigarettes huddling in the back for a pipe full of hash then walking down Crane past the comfortable middle class houses and well-manicured lawns towards Crescent Park under the hot hot Winnipeg sun (damn fine summers every day deep blue skies and brilliant sun) carrying the 24 between us and talking shit like old friends do,

"My old man just doesn't get it, he just doesn't fucking get it!" I said,

'What do you mean?...damn beer's fucking heavy, here, let's trade hands…"

"He doesn't get it, he doesn't get why I have long hair, he doesn't get my friends, my music, my attitude, my entire outlook on life completely escapes him man, he's fucking nuts!"

"My old man's a drunk…"

"Yeah, I know, that's some rough shit"

'So where'd you get that 1960's leather jacket man?"

"Ha ha ha, cool, isn't it? My brother gave it to me, and it IS from the sixties"

"Fucking parents, who needs 'em"

"Hear, hear…let's sit down and have a smoke…"

And we sat our lazy long hair asses on the curb lit smokes and looked up at the idiot sun…

Three hours later we were in the park by the river with the whole gang, Nazzie doing his thing telling us about the new drum progression he just figured out all manic energy taut like piano wire, then there was Joe little muscular guy with a Japanese father and an Italian mother smoking his corn-cob pipe full of hash drinking his Extra Old Stock beer real raunchy shit strong as hell, my cousin Max with that short powerful build and his sad kind eyes wild tough-ass attitude laughing continually till you pissed him off no one fucked with Max as he kissed Cindy she looking beautiful long long brown hair cut straight just above those intellectual eyes curiously grim man, and Judy by my side shoulder length curly hair brown and thick big blue eyes sweet-loving party girl wearing my leather jacket we were in teenage love man, Brenda was Cindy's best friend tall cool rock and roll girl with deep black hair all one length just brushing her shoulders pearl white skin wry smile nasty and beautiful she was paired up with Joe and they were in teenage-love, other schoolmates were there too about 50 or sixty

people in total, having a motherfucking ball man, shouting out with every fiber of our tortured beings whoooooooooo baaaaaaaaby!!! We were lit up like a pinball machine in overdrive, like a distorted guitar riff in E minor, like a volcano mind-fuck down the boulevard of angry dreams, Judy was a virgin and she thought I was too (I had lost my virginity by cheating on her) so we didn't fuck, but we did everything else you could imagine as she held tight affectionate as always and loving and considerate Judy was a class act all the way, I could have and should have done a lot worse, so we sat by the river and watched it move down the line and we laughed and smoked and got fucking crazy and there was the Paddlewheel Queen a huge cruiser that took people for a city tour on the water, they came by every night and every night we hollered and cheered them and they cheered back and it made our moment and we were in the middle of all that teenage insanity that is never forgotten, things being tough and sad and beautiful at the same time, bonfire reaching for the sky there goes Ross howling at the moon with all his sadness, and Nazzie climbing trees, and Joe sitting there laid-back-cool, and Max with Cindy on his arm downing beer like water, and Cindy herself making us laugh with her wigged-out all-intelligent personality and Brenda flirting with everyone looking nasty-sex-romp baby, Judy smiling at me blowing kisses in the bonfire wind, fight breaks out, fists are thrown, blood stains the night, me and Max immediately breaking it up, younger kids duking it out over a

girl, always a girl, then we heard the sirens, saw the flashlights, fucking pigs man, everyone started running in all directions…

3.

Cigarettes were a dollar and in those days we bought beer and cigs with no questions asked and no I.D. necessary, so I sat in my backyard at 1129 Waller Street and smoked thinking of this day when I first moved back from Italy, just two years prior to this story, tough jock pushed me in hallway, big fucking jarhead with python biceps, guess he thought I was the new kid from a different country, push that little fucker around right? He guessed wrong, I took a few shots, he gave a few, I gave a few more quick lightning jabs to the mouth and that fucker backed off and from then on in I was untouchable, truth be told in a full-fledged fist-fight he would have killed me but my personality and my aggressiveness and all around attitude intimated the shit out of him, lucky for me…finished the cigarette as my old man pulled up in the driveway and the second, the second he gets out of the car he's fucking screaming at me, and I scream back, and the neighbors see it, and the gods are crying over it, and the universe is howling, and we continue and continue and continue…

4.

Listening to The Doors flipping out on acid in my basement smoking hash and staring at a Jimi Hendrix poster the night was done, 2 in the morning, still tripping big time, had a few beers left from the party and was working on them, "Light My Fire" from The Doors came on, I swear I could see Jimi moving, I saw him bending the notes, I saw him twirl in the rain, I saw him smile sadly, the keyboard solo came on and my head went loco, I saw colors, random at first, then they melded into shapes of musicians playing various instruments, saw Jimi on guitar (but it wasn't really him), saw someone blowing the sax, saw a black guy playing the piano, saw a bass player on fire, literally, as he teased that fucking thing, eyes closed I was more alive than I had ever been with eyes open, the shapes and bright lights were never-ending and I knew from that moment on that our minds are not what we think they are, that the world isn't what we see, that existence is subjective and that all answers are inside, the colors went on and on and on, and she kissed me like it was the end of the world…

People are strange…we used to cut school and hang out at my place in the mornings make the afternoon bell just in time for Miss Brock's English class full of marijuana and teenage hormones running wild her mini-skirts a savage blessing Donna

and Shannon sitting around looking pretty and superior, the girls that hung with us then went to another school called Arthur A. Leach along with Max, ours was called Pembina Crest, Max was the connection that brought those girls to our neighborhood after the incident with Shannon and Donna and those jarhead jocks, so during the day it was the old group of girls, straighter and a bit snobbier and better adjusted, and at night it was the rock and roll chicks Judy and Cindy and Brenda and a score of others, raunchy young bad-assed girls that somehow managed to stay out all night with us and do drugs and get drunk and listen to Led Zeppelin and The Clash and AC/DC and all the other crazy shit that comes with it, the Fort Garry boys had met their match with those girls and it was mad-magic and thunderbolts man, it was love-struck lies in the darkened sun, it was Alvin Lee on a guitar-burst of tremendous love and lightning-speed-highway-stars, guitar licks up and down your body, warm kisses in the electrified gutter, savage blasts from the forlorn rock and roll memories, toothless smiles at the afternoon blues-jam, electric tingle between your thighs, barefoot ecstasy running rampant slow-easy afternoon blue skies so luvly it hurts,

it was green-eyes touching you softly,
it was me and you doing the slow-easy mambo
and the indifferent red light moaning in the
background to the
lust-rhythim and the

screaming unbearable happiness…

So we were at my place smoking the morning away, Ross, Joe, Nazzie, Judy, myself and a steady stream of other school buddies in and out of the place all morning long the stereo blasting The Velvet Underground into the neighborhood streets, then some Dire Straits and Led Zeppelin, the new Clash record and on and on, steady stream of smoke hovering around the room we took turns talking about certain things that were bothering us, certain things we liked, and we laughed and laughed and for those few hours felt alright like we belonged somewhere man, all of us with huge family problems and the usual teenage bullshit, Judy had an abusive father, Cindy's old man was a cop and a nasty one at that continually busting her up over sweet fuck-all, Nazzie's old man was a cop also and a good guy but a drunk as well, Joe actually had a very normal family who seemingly got along well, parents were liberal, older sister was hot and intelligent and open-minded, Joe was alright and was the happiest and most positive of us all, and a fuck of a pot smoker, whoa, Judy and I retreated to a corner as Ten Years After blasted from the stereo and she started talking,

"Hmmmm…" Short sweet kisses "it's one month today that we started going out…" She said,

"Really?"

"Prick"

“Well sorry, I’m not keeping track, you know…too busy having a good time with you…”

“Oh, you’re a piece of work, ha ha ha ha, no wonder your friends call you the snake, ha ha ha ha ha”

“Hey, I can only be me”

“So you keep saying…any chance we can sneak away from the gang later?”

“You bet baby, we’ll go to the park, have a few beers, steal a six-pack and go into the bush…remember the path?...leads to the river?”

“How can I forget, you put your hands down my pants there for the first time”

“Ha ha ha ha….wanna disappear there?”

“Hmmmmmm” Sweet kisses, warm little jabs “No place better…I like you soooooo much, Ziggy”

“Ditto…listen, how are things with the parents?”

“Fuck them…I don’t want to talk about it…later, ok?”

“No problem…”

Someone put on “Saturday Night’s Alright For Fighting”, which was Judy’s favorite song and she jumped and started jiggling those thighs to that groovy seventies beat those terri-cloth shorts clinging to her ass ripe like a peach tits bouncing up and down and that triangle between her legs thrust forward calling me loudly and a few other girls joined in the dance and Elton had us as we burst forward Tequila blasts straight from hell, so me and Judy ended up on that path leading to the river

laid on the grass kissing and moaning and rubbing each other under a ton of stars surrounded by bush and trees and the sounds of small things in the night and the distant traffic, occasional car horn, faint siren, a holler here and there (probably from our gang), but all distant and unreal to us as I wrapped my lips around her right nipple and rolled my tongue around and her hips arched and my teenage clumsiness working in the right direction as I kept tonguing her breasts she made those crying sounds and her stomach went up and down her ribs protruding out of that small body, large smile she was digging this full-time baby, I unbuttoned her pants and we wiggled them down to her ankles my hand reaching inside her underwear she lets out a deeper moan as I penetrate and a large breath is expelled, hmmmmmmm, and I'm massaging her wet mound and we're clumsily grinding into each other moving in this awkward rhythm that somehow works just fine, her hand in my pants she circles my cock and starts moving up and down the shaft and I'm seeing bright lights man, fucking hell motherfucker, I'm on my back and she's rubbing and yanking and moaning and my tongue is reaching out for every bit of flesh coming its way, beautiful warm summer night our bodies hot and inexperienced and restless and perfectly geared up for this, perfect time, perfect partner, perfect weather not a breeze in sight and Judy so goddamned lovely and gentle and kind and her warm wet tongue caressing me all over top to bottom, we were in teenage-love man…

5.

My old man had decided to take me out for dinner to a corner steakhouse and we actually got along alright talking about Italy and our shared memories, not with any tenderness or affection, oh no, that wasn't the old man's way, but for him something like this was a gigantic leap and I appreciated it, y'see this separation between us wasn't entirely his fault, he was trying as much as a stubborn southern Italian can suddenly thrust into single parenthood, he left me a bit of money every day, he had a laundry system set up, food was sparse but he left me money for that, so he joked about the shitty food here in Canada compared to Italy, the lack of culture and refinement, I disagreed being a proud Canadian, but laughed it off not wanting any bullshit and we went for a drive around the neighborhood in complete silence which is something he had always done, complete withdrawal man, the continuing and never-ending internal journey (a habit I've picked up), he dropped me off at home and took off somewhere, where's he always going I wonder?

I went for the phone, as planned, called Joe,

"Yeah…"

"Joe…"

"Uh-huh…"

"Everything cool?"

"It's all cool…they're here"

"And what about the girls?"

"You mean, our girls, or the ones here?"

"Well, both.."

"Our girls think we're at Cinema 3 watching that AC/DC movie....the other ones are right here drinking wine and getting high, ha ha ha ha"

"Fucking rights, my man!...what do they look like, they hot?"

"Oh yeah man, and they're easy"

"I'm on my fucking way, we alright for the drugs and booze?"

"Tons"

"See ya in ten"

And I moved on into the street under the thick trees and the hot summer night on my way to perform a dastardly act of infidelity without guilt of any kind, like the perfect bastard that I was...

Fort Garry was all bays and inlets and small parks and large trees and green grass everywhere and train tracks that ran right through the neighborhood as far as the eye could see, and on the other side of Pembina Highway were the richer houses and the golf courses and Crescent park on the Red River where we bush-partied all summer long and got high and got laid and laughed at the moon, so I walked down the tracks after school with Nazzie feeling that teenage angst wrapped around me like a blanket and we talked Nazzie trembling looking pale and sallow,

"What's up buddy?" My arm around him,

"Just feeling the crash man, you know?"

"The crash?"

"Yeah, too much partying, too much bullshit at home…"

He popped a few pills, offered me some,

"What are those?"

"Valium…."

"What do they do?"

"They just relax you man, older people take them when they can't sleep"

"What the fuck, you going to sleep?"

"No, no man, they get you high too, kinda lazy and real mellow"

"Nah, I'll pass"

"Okay"

"Here, give me a few…you're starting to worry me man with all that shaking"

"No, I'll be alright…it's fucking hard to see my old man so taken over from booze….he's a good guy, you know?"

"Yeah, he's the best, man, we all love him"

"He pushed my mom into the wall last night…"

"Jesus, fuck…"

"He didn't hurt her, it was nothing extreme, but he cried and drank for hours after that…I could hear him from my room all night"

"Fuck man…that's some serious shit"

"…life fucking sucks!"

"…listen, my old man works until 11 tonight, wanna hang out?"

"Can't…gotta go home…you know…"

"Okay Nazz…I'll talk to you later, alright?"

I watched him move away from me shoulders hunched uneven long strides I loved him with those sad shoulders and torn leather jacket blue runners spray-painted red alright brother, followed the tracks picking up the occasional stone and throwing it in no particular direction then I spotted Shannon crossing the street carrying her books, "Hey you crazy rock and roll chick!" I shouted out,

She stopped and looked around then she spotted me, I paused, she waved me in and I moved forward at a leisurely trot like I had all the time in the world,

"Hey" I said,

"Ziggy, how the fuck have you been?"

"Good, need some help with those books?"

"Nah, nothing I can't handle"

"So?"

"Yeah, that's what I should be saying to you"

"What do you mean?"

"You and your gang are pretty fucking infamous, everyone talks about you guys"

"But shunned by the mainstream, ha ha ha ha ha"

"Ha, ha ha ha…yeah, I suppose…you're too ugly for the mainstream" She laughs,

"Yeah, no argument" I laugh too, "Still going out with Dave?"

"Yep"

"Why?"

"Hey, he's my man, he's alright"

"Okay okay, ha ha ha, I seem to remember you telling me how unhappy you were at least 7 months ago.."

"Well things are never perfect, but-"

"-perfect my ass Shannon, you're 16 years old, what the fuck you hanging around with this guy for?"

"What do you mean?"

"You're not happy with this stupid fuck."

"-Hey!" Interrupting me,

"Everyone sees it Shannon, what the hell?"

"He's a good guy, c'mon…"

"He's a fucking goofball man"

"I suppose I should go for someone like you?"

"What the fuck does that mean?"

"Mister cool, leather jacket, long hair, rock and roll, where the hell are you going to be at 40?"

"40? Who gives a fuck about 40?"

"Look, let's sit down for a sec, got a cigarette?"

"Yeah, sure"

And we sat on the tracks as I lit two smokes and we looked around feeling the cool breeze of lonely happiness and separation…she smiled and my heart melted and I smiled back tapped her on the thigh meaning, "it's okay, it's alright",

"Got any pot?" She said,

"Got a roach, almost half a joint"

"Are you saving it?"

"Yeah, for this moment right here"

She smiled sadly and inhaled and passed it to me and we smoked in silence on the train tracks in the middle of the Canadian prairies in the middle of all that adolescent separation silver and gold sentiments and us being so close once and now so distant and Shannon so pretty with her working class understanding, Hello Shannon, I'm Ziggy, how is your life?

"Too bad about the fight" She said "With Barry and those guys…and us…"

"Fucking jocks"

"C'mon Zigg, it's not that easy"

"We started nothing with those fucking idiots"

"I know, I know, they felt threatened by you guys"

"Threatened?...c'mon, fucking jarheads…"

"Yeah, you guys have long hair, you use drugs, you sit on street corners, you fuck around with the chicks, THEIR chicks sometimes.."

"What's this "their chicks" crap?"

"Oh c'mon, you guys were just as territorial as they were, don't give me any bullshit Ziggy"

"Okay, okay, you're right…maybe we were both wrong, I don't know…but what's with the anti-long-hair bullshit, what is this, the 1940's?"

"Yeah, I know, ain't it sad?...hey, pass me that joint, ha ha ha..."

"Here you go..."

"I haven't smoked pot since the last time I hung out with you guys"

"Wow, that's a long time...you alright?"

"Yeah, don't tell anyone, but I always liked smoking grass, ha ha ha ha"

"Cool baby, cool"

There was a silence between us, not uncomfortable at all, just a space in time...

"We had fun, didn't we?" She said,

"...sure..."

The joint was done and it was somewhere around 5 o'clock, dinner time for the working class, Shannon smiled and stood up smoothed out her jeans and went on her way as I watched her ass jiggle away from me, bounce bounce bounce down those desperate train tracks me moving in the opposite direction always and forever and I saw the sun go down to its knees, I saw the ramshackle parade close down just before dawn, I saw the one-legged shark say goodbye in the murky love-morning, I saw the final hour begging for more, saw the winter fringe-dwellers kayak down the frozen landscape, now listen all you people to what I have to say,

ain't nothing permanent and happy,

ain't nothing sad and desperate...

6.

There was this little park in a back alley just down from the 7-11 where we hung out on mellow nights, back-alley-park we called it, no booze just large amounts of Maryjane and cool conversations small apartment building just across the lane tenants sitting out back aware of the whole thing yet not a single call to the cops man, no problems whatsoever, different times, different times, and we usually hung out till about 10:30 or 11 then walked home in the fading sun night coming down beautiful and desperate, and on week-ends we'd hit Crescent Park and bush-party the night away in the screaming light of our bonfire madness or we'd go to a house party where some shit or another would usually happen and we'd go fucking wild man, crazy-ass electricity flowing through the room violent and undeniable, Ross, Max, Nazzie and myself were the leaders, the wildest of the bunch, but besides it all we were good kids man living under the rock and roll shadow and I took the motto and lifestyle seriously and truly didn't give a fuck about anything...

But it was a mellow night at back-alley-park that I was musing on...Ross and Joe talking in one corner about music and guitar players, Nazzie, Cindy, Brenda and Max sat on the grass in a semi-circle laughing about something, Brenda jumping up and down...me and Judy huddled against the fence on the other side of the park soft kisses in the sun-go-down beauty, my hand on her soft thighs plump and long and fleshy, we're smiling in

each other's arms saying nothing just swaying in the summer breeze golden moments at dusk like these never forgotten thinking I could do that forever, thinking that life would never change and that change can go fuck itself, unwilling to accept the unavoidable ending of all things, the constant state of flux called life, the inevitable change that all things have to go through in order to achieve individuation, no, no way anyhow, not ever, I ran my fingers through the grass the leaves cool to my touch, Judy laid her head on my chest and closed her eyes, a siren echoed in the distance then faded, a sudden stillness came into the night where everything went quiet, or seemed to, I could feel Judy breathing on my chest and her heart beating slowly against me, happy moments at back-alley-park as the dusk settled in and we leaned forward and breathed in the moment…

7.

Toughest guy in school was Harry Kruger big fucking guy with natural muscles biceps like anaconda tombstones wore a brown leather jacket all scuffed and worn out he was one of us but not around as often cuz there was something strange going on at his house, something about his old man, he never talked about it and no one asked but rumor was the old man was dying and Harry was taking care of him, at the age of 16 this guy was already an alcoholic, unlike the rest of us who were partiers, drinkers, he was a bonafide drunk, I shit you not, but we loved him cuz he was a lovable drunk, and cuz he was the toughest guy in school, maybe in the neighborhood, or even the adjoining ones (there was Waverley Heights where Max and the girls all lived, Fort Richmond on the other side of the tracks where our hated rival Acadia High was, Fort Rouge just south past the Pembina Underpass where I had grown up with intermittent moves back to Italy soul sacrifice here I come!) so Harry sat with me watching a girl's volleyball game, we always made time to leer at Shannon and Donna in those tiny terri-cloth shorts and tight t-shirts jumping up and down and left and over the fat at the back of the thighs jiggling just right and the tits up and down in some kind of strange death-sex-march, Donna's long blond hair and Shannon's shoulder length hazel curls flowing like red red wine casting shadows around the room making us all crazy man, wind us up and BANG like the atom bomb on

your front doorstep, whoa, Harry talked about his favorite Led Zeppelin guitar solo and why he hates punk and why The Beatles suck and why The Stones are the best rock band of all time followed closely by AC/DC and Led Zeppelin is the most accomplished and on and on and on and on, I would listen, then laugh, then listen and smack his shoulder and laugh and listen and bop to his particular rhythm then stop to point out Donna kneeling down in a certain way only to jump upwards and spike the volleyball muscles in her thighs flexing with timeless precision as a bead of sweat trickled down our brows, or Shannon adjusting the line of her shorts around the thighs then slightly bouncing up and down waiting for the serve from the other side her eyes focused and alert, man oh man, then Harry would continue and I would continue and he respected me to no end this muscle bound pussycat and I him even though beyond classic rock we completely disagreed on music, but who gives a fuck, right? Game over…Shannon and Donna waved at us and moved to the locker rooms as we exhaled and smiled and felt satisfied for the moment, Harry pulls out one of those huge 7-11 drinks and gives me a sip turns out there's vodka in there, fuck me, "Doesn't smell" he said "let's get the hell out of here" out the back door we go, Joe's there, with Nazzie and Ross (acting crazy getting the laughs all around) school was right on Pembina Highway so we saw a bus pull up and out came Max with another guy smaller than him, turns out it was our childhood friend Ibrahim, a Trinidadian fellow with thick black

hair and dark skin who had been among our best friends since we were 5 years old,

"Jesus!" I said "Ibby, where the fuck you coming from?"

We shook hands and hugged,

"Just moved back to town, and right in the middle of Waverley Heights down the block from Max, FUCK ME!!!"

"No, FUCK ME! Whoooo, this is fucking great, you in school, or what?"

"Nah, I failed, I'm done for the year, going to Leach next year with Max here"

"Maybe I should join you there?"

"You're going to Vincent Massey with the rest of these clowns, ain't ya?"

"You're looking at the first guy in history to purposely fail a school year" Said Max to Ibby

"Let me guess" said Ibby in my direction "you had to make a point"

We laughed, "Yeah" I said, "something like that"

"Ziggy you Italian prick, gonna introduce your friend, or what?" Shouted Ross,

"Ibby, these are the boys, go nuts"

And they shook hands and exchanged names and started laughing and we walked to the fence at the back of the schoolyard and sparked up Ibby hitting it off immediately with the boys (him and Joe later became great friends) and right at that moment a jock tough guy went walking by looking at us

and moving away briskly…we knew each other…and he hadn't forgotten…

8.

We'd started doing acid quite frequently and had even gotten into the habit of doing it in the morning just before home-room, just a few of us of course only the hardcores, me, Nazzie, Ross and Max but Max was at that other school, so this particular morning we had tongued a hit of orange phoenix each beautiful little orange paper squares with black symbols on them supposed to be phoenixes which just looked like shit to me, walked into the hallways with the paper on our tongues and during home-room lecture we were still chewing on them smiling at each other waiting for that beautiful storm to come, Donna was wearing a pair of jean shorts runners and white ankle socks and I couldn't keep my eyes off her thighs, from where she was sitting I had the angle- view her bronzed thigh looking enormous and juicy and a gift from the gods, she turned in my direction and I quickly looked away Ross noticing the whole thing stifling that crazy-ass laugh of his, home-room over, the day began…

Walking the halls that day was an adventure somewhere between heaven and hell and pure sexless bliss, it started crawling up on me during gym class man I was throwing that fucking ball with lighting deadly speed, whoa, said the coach, whoa there young fella, ha ha ha I laughed ha ha ha (dumb shit), ha ha, okay coach, moving right along, he laughed with me in his infinite ignorance not suspecting a damn thing and me thinking of the Sex Pistols and high-energy rock and roll cutting a clear swath through the face of the universe and existence coming to its fucking knees and the sun frowning in the brilliant moonlight riot police out in full force drinking gutter-love running for their gin-soaked lives branded by another hellish pawn in the Ska Roots slam-dance flying to one end of the dance floor after an elbow to the head I wanna riot me screaming at the brutal reality hey Ziggy, hey Ziggy, oh yeah yeah, sure, what's up man, it was Ross,

"I'm starting to freak out" He said quietly, but even as he spoke he was restraining a smile,

"Me too, me too" Huge fucking smile on my face,

"Okay, okay, let's move on, move on"

"Alright, alright, stop pushing" Suppressing laughter,

"Okay, asshole, ha ha ha"

Gym class over me and Ross ran outside as fast as we could and lit smokes feeling the tingling and the strange sensations running up and down our bodies and the shadows started flashing out of the corner of my eyes, what the fuck's that, scalp tingling, bitter taste in mouth, eyes starting to bug out, smile from ear to ear, Ross looking gigantic and bizarre huge head, smokes done we ran back inside everything moving in a slightly different time-beat shimmery and almost unreal, what a day I thought, what a day, then I saw a clock and noticed it was only 11:a.m., jesus man, fucking hell...

By the time school was done I was about halfway through the acid trip which meant the laughing stage, Ross had taken off and I was just entering my yard laughing about something inconsequential and seeing all sorts of colors and shades all around me when my old man looks out the window and waves me in, Buddha help me, he's all smiles and he's talking away in Italian about all sorts of things anger coming to the surface only to be swallowed back down then he's talking about my mother betraying him then waving it off and trying to smile and me thinking, why does he have a fucking red orb surrounding his head, what the hell is that shadow in the corner, then suppressing laughter cuz his Italian's sounding really funny man, a few times the laughter bursting out but quickly suppressed and the old man not seeming to mind, then he starts talking about renovating the basement for me and changing certain things around the house making extensions here and there, what the hell I'm thinking, what the hell, man I started seeing all sorts of things moving around that kitchen, nothing very clear but fragments and shapes and shadows and everything looking funny and everything amplified as he finally says goodnight and flips me ten bucks and I move downstairs as fucking fast as I can what a trip baby, I sat down and the second my ass touched the couch there was a knock on my window, made me jump three feet into the air almost hit my head on the low basement ceiling, curtain open I notice Max grinning from

ear to ear and a slight look of panic on his face, he had dropped the acid at the same time as me in the morning and went through the same bullshit I'm sure at his school, I opened the door and in he came trippin' out and wiry and red-faced and we start laughing and laughing and laughing as he pulls out a bottle of Rye, smokes and a small bottle of Coke, whoa, whooooooo, he points upstairs referring to my old man,

"He's alright, watching t.v."

"I'm going to say hello"

"What, now?"

"Why the fuck not? He's my uncle, ain't he?"

"Yeah, but now? With the acid and everything?"

"Oh fuck that, no problem man, I'll be right back, just a quick hello"

Okay, so he went up and I sat back and mixed a rye and coke took one sip and Max came running back downstairs,

"What the hell??? That was fast!"

"I told ya, he's watching the tube, MASH, it was all dark, he couldn't tell shit…he was good"

"Cool man…"

"Make me a drink, I'm going to roll a joint…that's good, not too much coke man, whoa, whoa, too much…okay, that's good…cheers"

"What a fucking day man!"

"You're telling me…I was fucking freaking out in gym class man!"

"Me too, ha ha ha ha, you should have seen Ross with his fucking long arms, he looked like a fucking ape running around the gym, he was tripping over people, it was fucking nuts, ha ha ha ha…"

"Ha, ha ha ha ha ha"

And we laughed at nothing and everything cuz that's where the LSD wanted us at the moment, pointing at the most ridiculous of things and letting forth a thunderous raucous bellow,

"I love this part of the acid trip man, my guts bursting, oh shit, stop making me laugh…"

"You know Max, I'm thinking of telling Judy I cheated on her"

Everything serious all of a sudden we stop dead…Max looking at me deeply…then he roars into laughter,

"Get the fuck out of here, ha ha ha ha"

And I'm laughing too and it continues like this and I'm looking at those large arms of his that barrel chest he was short and stocky close to the ground I couldn't imagine anyone taking him in a fight, not anyone, but what an absolutely congenial personality, what an easy person to like man, what easy laughter came out of his mouth, easy laughter but the sadness always there just under the surface, like me, like me a result of parental divorce hormones gone crazy sex drugs and rock and roll struck by the life-surprise, by the sudden twisting of reality, laughing laughing the one-eyed nun on her knees begging for

more, the forlorn sinner giving all he can, the drug-addled popstar choking on his own ego then the acid trip takes another turn and the downslide begins and suddenly all the booze which you had downed with such great ease hits you in the fucking head and the marijuana's swimming in your brain and you're feeling a bit down wishing the whole thing was over and the talk turns serious and you're glad for friends and family and home and warmth,

"I don't know Zigg…" He said,

"What do you mean?"

"…I don't know man…I mean…"

"Yeah…I hear ya…"

So at around 11 or 12 bottle done acid trip coming down hard and sad we said goodbye on a school night and I watched my cousin walk out the door and I thought the world of him and us and everything that had contributed to this bizarre turn of events, two Italian boys born in Torino, Italy somehow ending up across the world in Canada dropping acid and wandering the streets of Fort Garry what a surreal experience, what an orgy-fest ordeal it all turned out to be, and the melancholy moment got me thinking about my mother and my brother back in Italy and my broken family and my misguided adventures I sat there feeling the darkness and the aloneness and the ultimate undeniable truth, moonlight laughter is sad and lonely …

9.

The old man started freaking out on me more and more talking all kinds of shit about my mother which didn't sit well with me at all, we had real nasty screaming matches man, real ugly and desperate and distant, once out that fucking door I buried it deep inside and the Ziggy everyone loved was in full view, I was alive and free and wild and I looooooooved a good time man, but my insides were twisted and full of anger and those close to me could see it, they saw the pale shadow hanging over my face, they saw the cold-distant dead-eye look, the early morning drug binge mind in overdrive shooting out ideas feelings bottled up anger sadness happiness mixing together in a deadly brainwave-explosion, so I was sitting in Miss Brock's class…

Almost over tic toc tic toc feeling particularly nasty started talking to Shannon during a lecture, started getting aggressive and insulting making all sorts of references to her idiot boyfriend and those ridiculous jock friends of hers, her eyes started to fill with water but she was defiant and proud, Miss Brock finally had enough,

"Ziggy!"

"Fuck off"

The class went dead silent and Miss Brock stood there almost in shock unable to speak,,,suddenly the bell rang…it was lunch hour…everyone jumped out of their chairs and headed for the

door…Miss Brock came right up to my desk and made a motion for me to stay…I saw Shannon glaring at me tears in her eyes as she walked out the door…Miss Brock went to the door and closed it softly…

"What the fuck, Ziggy???

I shrugged my shoulders,

"You're telling me to fuck off now?"

Again with the shoulders,

Her tone got softer,

"Ziggy, you can talk to me, you know that, right?"

"Sorry…"

"Apology accepted…do you want to talk?...is it something to do with Shannon?...you guys had that big fight…"

"Nah, she's alright…things at home are fucked…"

"I know…"

"And that's about all I'll say about that…"

'Okay, Ziggy…if you ever feel like shooting the shit…you know?"

"I know…still coming to the Kiss concert?"

"Of course…tickets go on sale next Saturday, right?"

"Yup…ummm, can I go now?"

"See ya…"

Walked out into the hall feeling low-down and dirty unpleasant thoughts racing through my mind but got sudden flash of a song called "Sweet Georgia Brown" played by Sydney Bechet, heard that clarinet sing-song go from one ear to the other with

astounding clarity hallways dead and silent a typewriter somewhere in the distance gym teacher walks by smiling I ignore him keep moving through the maze occasional student hunched over reading textbooks mostly quiet and cool and mind suddenly in easy-mode-wonder feeling reinforced somehow my internal optimism rising to the surface of its own volition, there was nothing I could do, my brain had decided to be happy, so I went with it and floated into that blue-cool place, that wonderstruck mind-fuck, that external eternal dance down the rust-covered petrol-emotion alleyways...

It was to be Nazzie, Ross, Joe, Max and myself, tickets went on sale at 7 a.m. at a large five story department store called Eaton's and we were going to do the rock and roll campout, had heard of the ritual for quite awhile but this was our first, rock and roll virgins you might say, we had enough money for the whole gang, flasks full of wine and pre-mixed Rye and Coke, a bag of grass and a gram of mushrooms each, whoa, I braced myself and we rode the bus downtown after ingesting the shrooms place packed with teenagers doing the same thing as us a bit subdued but this was the calm before the storm baby, it was in the very air around us electricity slithering around everything like a snake we met a few people shook hands the bus taking us over the Donald Bridge and into the heart of downtown Winnipeg everything kinda dark and strange on Broadway but once the corner was turned we saw that huge

fucking crowd, thousands of people circling the building security marching the sidewalks crowd just kinda spreading out over the downtown a sea of bodies scattered across various parking lots with barb-q pits all lit up and openly drinking in plastic cups the fuzz circling cautiously cuz as long as the cups were plastic they left you alone, heard a bottle smash down the street and off raced the coppers sirens and all, "whoooooooo-hoooo" shouted Nazzie, "jesus man, I feel fucking wired, I feel GREAT!"

"Fucking rock and roll man, fuck me" Said Ross looking out at the crowd "welcome to the big leagues boys"

So we moved in and Ross immediately started talking to people man shaking hands smiling offering marijuana we were in the thick of things Max was laughing and singing and chatting up the girls, Nazzie always wired and crazy kind-hearted to a flaw, for a second it looked like our kind-hearted friend was about to shove a beer bottle down this fucker's throat who kept saying, "women love my fucking 12 inch man!", "I love to eat gash baby, and those fucking cunts love to eat me, whoa!!!!" but it all slowed down and nothing-doing baby cuz no one wanted to fight at that moment (at that moment mind you, there's more to come) cuz the mushrooms were taking hold and we were perma-grinned rosy facing the world with a head full of drugs and a belly full of Rye and desperation and we could hear Jimi Hendrix coming from somewhere in the distance but sounding like it blasted right up against my ears and I asked the

boys if they felt the same, nods smiles yeah uh huh oh yeah more smiles, so that's where we sat…at the outer rim of a massive parking lot full of rowdy young passionate rock and rollers Eaton's building in full view group of boys and girls come right up to us carrying a crazy-ass huge fucking ghetto blaster (the one blasting Hendrix, "Who Knows"), uh-huh, the flasks are out and the night has taken on a magnificent almost blinding color, streetlights flashing orange, neon signs lit like Karnival, construction lights brilliant red, small fires scattered across the parking lot coming from the pits, car horns in the distance, Hendrix wailing the electric blues, shouts and laughter and macho challenges and the endless rock and roll uber–dance, scene bordering on wild but contained so far everyone concealing the booze and the drugs somewhat, cops hovering around the edges with furrowed brows and taut jaws but no problems , BANG heard a firecracker go off, no maybe a bottle rocket, then the streamer in the sky painting everything red blue and orange our faces lit up in multicolored wonder under the full hallucigenic effect of the mushrooms, foot patrol bolted in the direction of the blast, shit, whooooooo, jesus man wow dig this scene, and it continued like that till morning then slowly we started to hover around the building red-eyed and blurry crowd so packed in I was literally being carried by it shoulder to shoulder, I could see Ross towering over everyone getting pushed all over the place and swearing his head off, the rest of the boys were lost to me but I felt confident they were alright, I

had the money for the tickets looked like I was going in alone, voices started getting raunchier the sounds of violence all around us crowd starting to slow I found a spot right up against the building suddenly a beer bottle flew through the air and smashed on the ground right beside security, SMASH…another two followed in quick succession, BANG, SMASH…to the right of me a fight broke out one guy getting clobbered repeatedly in the head, fuck me man, didn't take long for the paddy wagons and the extra cops to show up and start busting heads man, this shit had turned serious and ugly there was an opening in front of the building where the cops all convened, few bottles thrown in that direction went smashing to the ground one of them was full and the beer formed a beautiful foamy stain on the cement, whoa, people were hauled into the wagons and the crowd responded with more shouts and tossed bottles, Ross had worked his way right beside me looking concerned and a bit freaked out but even with all this insanity around us I felt we were alright and a small smile formed on my face as a cop stood facing the crowd after throwing someone in the wagon,

"ALRIGHT, ANYONE ELSE HAVE A FUCKING PROBLEM, WE GOT LOTS OF WAGONS!...HUH?....ANYONE FUCKING ELSE?" Crowd went silent…we were stunned…who was this fucking creep with the balls of king kong?...a long haired guy walked right up to the cop, "what the hell is this?" said Ross, and I shit you not this fucking guy took a swing at the cop and they hit the street with

the long-hair giving the best of it, that was enough for us, we had found our hero, we screamed for the long-hair and if the reinforcements hadn't arrived that cop was his, so they haul him away as he waves and we cheer him on, whooooooooo, things seemed to calm down just a bit after that looked like we wanted our fucking tickets and had had enough of the song and dance, but still the music was loud, the people were crowded in and drunk and high and smiling angry man, so I was inched closer and closer to the front entrance Ross beside me grin spread from ear to ear, sun out in full force I glance backwards see Max, Nazzie and Joe hanging out on the second level of a parking lot directly across from us, they see me and wave their beer bottles in the air then put them down quickly as the cops look around, thumbs up baby, damn that door five feet away now, closer and closer then we're inside and amazingly the ticket booth is only ten feet away and we're there in no time tickets in hand for everyone, we fucking did it! We walked out into the blinding sun stumbling along suddenly tired as hell reach the other boys they're looking just like us, weak smiles all around we move forward inch by inch the next leg of this unexpected journey ahead of us as the bus pulls up we're inside saying nothing just looking out the windows the downtown buildings going by in a flash of gray and brown Ross asleep head tilted against the window then I felt it again, in the middle of all that tiredness and numbness and the down slide of a

mushroom trip all around me, I felt that smile reach my lips once again and it was alright man, alright…

10.

So the concert was up…thousands of people wearing Kiss make-up sticking their tongues out and lining up and passing refeer and while we're in the middle of it all here comes Miss Strock with a man-friend and sits right in front of us giving us the most subtle of smiles then turning away her man thick mustache and curly hair down to his shoulders, good for you Miss Strock the fucker was an anti-conformist, turns out her seat was right in front of me and I kept blowing marijuana smoke in her direction cloud enveloping her head time and time again and we're sipping from our wine flasks security everywhere and not a word said about the marijuana and the cigarettes and the wine flasks and the other drugs, can you imagine that happening today? First band was on, The Scorpions, unknown at the time uneventful kinda crappy jock-metal not my thing, then came Pat Travers Canadian hard rocker a little better, then that fucking Ted Nugent came in swinging on a loincloth could see the smile on Miss Strock's face and our whole gang howling and screaming at the top of our lungs, once Nugent was done and it was time for Kiss the entire arena was wasted and ready and willing and they came on and I felt the heat from the explosions on my forehead and Miss Strock's buddy lit a joint passed it to her and everything so fucking loud my ears started bleeding, or at least in the insanity it felt that way…

11.

When I think back on Judy it was her ability to fit into all situations so easily that stands out most and her absolute complete devotion to her man, or teenager in this case, she was used to shitty relationships with shitty men starting with her father all the way down to her last boyfriend, now I was no prize but in comparison I was a thing of beauty, I treated her like a queen man she was always by my side, always, keeping up drink for drink smoke for smoke, it was Ziggy and Judy all the way and we had become somewhat legendary in the neighborhood as a kool-kat couple that walked lazily down the street arm in arm cigarettes hanging from their lips black leather jackets sitting on street corners or laying in the park we were happy man, in the middle of all the bullshit we were happy…on this afternoon at my place we laid on my bed after a make-out session and we talked and talked and talked,

"I don't know how much more I can take it Judy, I really don't"

"Well what are you going to do Zigg? What can you do man?"

"Well there are some fucking things I can do, I refuse to feel helpless about anything"

"Okay Ziggy…"

"I can't stand him talking about my mother that fucking way and I tell him over and over again and he fucking does it over and over again, FUCK!"

"Well your old man doesn't drink, at least there's that"

"Does yours hit you?"

"Oh shit he hasn't actually hit me in a long time, but that threat is always there, you know?"

"Yeah…"

"He treats us all like shit Ziggy, he's a fucking freak….as soon as I'm legal, I'm out of there…would you live with me?"

"Sure…of course that would mean I'd have to get a job…ummmmm"

"Well you're going to have to someday Zigg"

"I always figured I'd do it with my music"

"Okay, I'll be your groupie girlfriend, we'll be happy, can you imagine?" Says it sadly,

"I can imagine"

"What's going to happen from here?"

"I don't know…have no fucking idea…"

I was on my back with Judy's head on my shoulder and I could feel her tears rolling onto my skin and the gentle sobbing and the never-ending sadness entering the room….

After Judy left I found myself sitting at back-alley-park with Joe and Brenda and Cindy, crazy fucking kids, they were talking all sorts of shit Cindy being the smartest you could tell early on this girl had brains to spare and she wasn't going to sit still for too long,

"Why do we need guys to feel complete?" She said,

"Or why do we need chicks I might add?" I said,

"Yes, exactly, why the hell do you need chicks?"

"I don't need one…" Said Joe smiling,

"….I want one" I said, finishing his sentence,

Brenda rolls her eyes as me and Joe laugh our stoned heads off, Cindy shakes her head restraining a smile herself,

"Fucking guys" said Brenda "Typical"

Then she grabs her tits and sticks her tongue out at us,

"So did you hear from Max?" Said Cindy,

"He'll be here…I think…his old man was giving him a hard time...about something"

"I actually had a great lunch with my mom the other day" Said Joe,

"Yeah, she's super cool" Said Brenda,

"We talked about school and shit and girls and what the fuck, you know?"

"I know I know" I said,

"Lookit at how big Joe's arms are getting" Said Brenda,

Joe had been working out and was looking pretty wild and tough and slick,

"Fuck that shit man, c'mon" Joe in typical easy-cool fashion,

"I feel relaxed man, like I could do this forever" And he stretched out in the sun on the grass smile on his face looking cool and easy-living,

"Very Japanese" Said Cindy referring to Joe,

We all laughed at that one, including Joe, ha ha ha ha, holidays in the sun baby, but if it got down Joe was a tough

motherfucker man, saw him nail a guy in the forehead once sending the fucker flying 10 feet in the air man, I shit you not, people left him alone and he left them alone, and the afternoon faded away and Ibby showed up with another childhood friend Italian bloke called Salvatore big black afro dark skin funny guy man, funny guy sitting around smoking that shit we thought was so good Columbian Gold they called it but it was nothing more than ditch weed tons and tons of seeds we used to put it through a strainer or sift the seeds out on an album cover with the edge of a cigarette pack, we rolled a joint each and sat there and talked and smoked them like cigarettes slowly and at our leisure and Salvatore making us laugh our goddamn guts out and Ibby talking about our childhood and me thinking laughing talking thinking laughing smoking smiling the endless lonesome blues out the edge of my crooked mouth firecracker wisdom written all over my face shaking Ibby's hand seeing the beginnings of his friendship with Joe unfold in a hazy cloud of undetermined synchronicity, and I swear I saw a cricket playing a violin, I saw a bloodhound snorting whiskey, I saw an old lizard on his front stoop singing country and western, heard Sidney Bechet blowing his horn, saw the wind cry Mary toothless meanderings on the deadly waterfront, the wind heavy in your hair train tracks rolling into the offset panorama skyline gray and dismal reel to reel horror show in the shadows of your mind, Peppe the lizard running down the summertime blues stumbling through your backyard magic man lethal injection to

the soul wandering minstrel in the urban reality sidewalk hooker slides down the lost-love boulevard, and I walked the streets under the full moon in no hurry to get home, in no hurry to get anywhere down and around the bays and inlets of Fort Garry and the night was still silent hot thick green everywhere landscape spotted with small parks and two or three different schoolyards with hockey rinks where the boys and girls huddled in the penalty boxes to smoke their cigarettes and their grass and to give their blow jobs and their teenage sex-capades remembered getting a blow job in a penalty box I was walking by at that moment, Andrea was her name one year younger short blond with thick curly hair flowing down her back and rivulets on her forehead going into her eyes man, big blue eyes and pouty lips teenage fat on her legs and ass well rounded young girl had seduced me in the halls at school, I hadn't even noticed her until she walked up to me after gym class in those terri-cloth shorts with the red stripe on the sides lightly tanned thighs all blushes and hips swaying faintly then we were in the box her mouth around my cock moving slowly up and down inexperienced and beautiful and worth fighting for, it was her that first turned me on to going down on women, I was lousy at it (still am) and she kept moaning and groaning and talking "no, no, no, not there, that's the wrong place, yeah, right there....okay, just move your head...a little...to the right...mmmmmmmkay...." When I got a good streak going she would squeeze my head between her thighs fiercely causing me

all kinds of pain and pleasure, "jesus, take it easy, urgggg, take it easy sister…jeez…" then get my head back in there and get the tongue in there, again she squeezes, "jesus!!!....urrrgggg, Andrea, what the…aggggg…take it easy with those fat thighs man…" back in there like the trooper I was she knocked me over and got that huge mass of blonde hair between my legs and started bopping and weaving going up and down up and down my hands caressing her hair and feeling that lion mane tickling my thighs her head jerking from side to side, then it was done….damn…so I sat in front of that penalty box remembering everything and wondering and looking at the moon and I went inside the box and lit a smoke still looking up at the sky full of stars and that hot Winnipeg night man the smell of freshly cut grass coming from somewhere, feeling sad but oddly alright with it, truly felt like I could handle anything that came my way, a delusion of the mind of course but that works too…

12.

That night at Crescent Park was beyond anything we had experienced there before, scattered across the park were many different parties of various sizes and of various age groups, you could look down the river bank and see the bonfires lining the shore and the ghetto blasters were out different types of music heard echoing through the park we had tons of batteries and tons of tapes ranging from The Ramones to Led Zeppelin to Joe Jackson to early Kiss and there were at least a hundred people in our party alone, had to be around one thousand all told and me Ross and Nazzie bouncing from party to party keeping our home base close but never staying at any place for too long and Judy partying it up she had brought her tent that night telling her parents she was sleeping at a friend's place along with Joe and Brenda and I had decided I was spending the night outdoors too and she had pitched it right by the river and we went in and out in and out meeting kissing having a beer then separating then doing it all over again there were a group of older guys and gals at the far end of the park and they were listening to reggae, Jimmy Cliff, "They Harder They Come", we started dancing and doing the reggae bop and an older girl swayed and moved in rhythm with me and Ross and Nazzie had girls as well and the older guys were a pleasure man, all mellow and smiles and marijuana-lovely and my girl blond and tall and groovy dressed like a hippie she was two grades ahead of me

and I had seen her everyday for two years and had never spoken a word to her and the beat moved us closer together and we gyrated happy as hell man and this moment of light and beauty burned forever in my brain, on our way back to our neck of the woods passing bonfires and young people drinking and getting high we lose Nazzie somewhere along the way keep moving saying the whole time how cool that reggae scene was and how we're going to take the others there and wow man, jesus hell man, cool shit grooving baby like a rolling stone, "FUCK ME!" screams Ross, opens a beer and downs it, stumbles, regains his balance, laughs, throws me a beer can alright baby, so we gather our crew, the main members anyway and drag them towards the reggae scene only to find nothing there man, last remnants of the bonfire fading away scattered beer bottles and cans all over the place and suddenly I felt the sadness creep up my spine and I looked at my crew and I saw it on their faces as well staring at the dying embers and the wind blowing through Cindy's hair and Judy almost in tears and Max defiant but feeling it man, there was a loud blast behind us and a chorus of shouts wooooooo, what the fuck baby, we moved past the bushes and saw a huge bonfire shooting up twenty feet in the air horde of people throwing wooden picnic tables, chairs, logs, beer cases into it and in the middle of all that we see Nazzie jumping in and out of that fucking thing, whoooooeee, crazy fucker, he was wearing a huge cowboy hat which caught on fire without him noticing until someone pointed it out and he flipped

it into the air a beautiful flaming arch landing somewhere in the bush, "jesus" I said "we're going to start a fucking forest fire!", and as that last word came out of my mouth the spotlights and sirens and fucking pigs came running into the bush man, Joe immediately ran for Nazzie and me and Max telling the girls to go ahead, "we'll grab the tent, meet you at the far entrance, hurry!", so me and Max navigating that insane crowd and spotlights and fires and cops and shouts and music we reach the tent and get it the fuck out of the ground damn quick Max packing it up as fast as possible notice the cops moving in our direction "move baby!" I shout and off we go man weaving through those bushes up and around like Olympic sprinters youth in full bloom reach the far entrance see the gang waiting for us, Ross comes running up,

"You assholes alright?"

We nod catching our breath leaning forward, laugh laugh laugh, Ross and Nazzie and the rest take off home, Joe, Max, Brenda, Judy and myself continue on our track heading for Waverley Heights where Max and Judy lived, "I know a perfect spot to pitch that tent for the night" said Max, "You staying for the night man?" I said, "No, I'll point the way, c'mon, it's a half an hour walk, got any beer left?" "Lots" I hand him one and we pass it around as we reach the train tracks and follow those straight lines far into the night all of us feeling tough and mean and alive and Judy defiant lips pursed brow furrowed the dark

reality calling us deeper and deeper into the heart of Saturday night…

"This is the spot?" I said,

"Yeah, isn't it wild?"

I looked around…we were in the back of the high school Max and Judy went to, it was called Arthur Leach High, the building being spitting distance from the tent,

"What the fuck Max? You don't think the cops are going to wonder why there's a fucking tent pitched in
the schoolyard?"

"No, no, it's perfect, see, you can't see it from the street cuz of that hill, and it's Saturday, hell, Sunday morning, who the fuck's going to notice?"

"Alright you crazy fucker…"

"Okay, give me a joint, I have to go man"

"Anything else?"

"Hurry up, it's fucking late, don't fuck around"

I hand him a joint and he waves and is off, Judy comes out of the tent big damn smile on that gorgeous face,

"This is fucking great baby, whoooooo!"

I went inside saw Joe and Brenda kinda crashed in a corner bottle of Jack between them tent large enough to sleep four Judy curled up to me and we huddled in a corner listening to Bob Marley's greatest hits smoking grass sipping on beer smiling and sleepily kissing and rubbing and hearing the night

go silent Judy's breathing slowing down and everyone asleep except for me arm around my teenage love beer to my lips music soft and softer head goes fuzzy Judy curls up closer and purrs and moans and my mind goes dark and we remember no more…

13.

I didn't go home that night…or the night after…or the night after that…I had decided to run away from home, slept on top of Crane high school one night, in the park the other, and in an abandoned shack just down the street from my house on the third night where muscle-bound Harry had given me a case of beer and a hit of acid and I had consumed and hallucinated and felt down and low and alone and very sad…

Stayed away from home for another three nights sleeping wherever the hell I could and on the final night went home and the old man freaking out more than ever, veins popping out on his forehead whole fucking neighborhood hearing this drama threatening to send me to reform school saying I'm just like my mother and blah blah blah and somewhere inside my defiant soul I could feel that this was as much my fault as it was his, and that he was trying but it was coming out all wrong, and the same with me man, an awkward social situation between two individuals who didn't know how to reach out, I went to bed that night feeling lousy and tired starving but not for food, so school ended the following week and I failed like planned but

the old man knew this was coming and he tried a softer approach speaking to me calmly (but anger visible under the surface) saying we have to buckle down and try harder and I said okay, yes, uh-huh, actually meaning it for that moment but forgetting about it as soon as I walked out the door cuz it was fucking SUMMER man, and I was going to live it crazy man, real crazy, ended up stealing a car just a week after school ended, listen…

…not that I knew how to hotwire or that I was an actual decent thief of some kind but we had been hanging out at this chick's place and she had showed us where the keys to her old man's car were kept threatening that if he didn't quit drinking she would steal his fucking car one day and run away from home, so it came that her old man was gone out of town for two weeks leaving the car behind and of course I came up with the idea….just for a joyride I said, but the girl in question got wind of the plot and said that we could drive it around town for the entire two weeks as long as we filled up the tank, her old man wouldn't know jack, alright baby, here we go…and that's what happened man, Christ, none of us knew how to fucking drive, not to mention the drugs we were on and the booze and the teenage angst and all that shit, very very dangerous living as I drove that little Pinto into downtown rush hour traffic and Judy in the front seat panicking, and Ross in the back trying to keep her calm and Max keeping vigilance, Joe, Nazzie, Ibby smoking pot and laughing but on the edge man, on the edge, my battle

plan was simply to do everything the car in front of me did, and I had never driven a car before but somehow managed to pull it off wheeling away from downtown and back to the calm Fort Garry streets finding a spot under a tree in the shade and spending the afternoon getting high and laughing wondering if /when the axe was going to fall but it never fell and we did this routine for the whole two weeks filling the gas tank on the last day just a block from the car's garage when we spot Max and Cindy hanging out by a corner store smoking cigarettes (was me, Judy, Ibby and Joe in the car), we wave them in Max insisting he take the wheel placing Cindy between us lovely tanned thighs in those blue terri-cloth shorts white ankle socks huge fucking brown eyes, Max takes the wheel and peels out right in front of a restaurant grinning at Cindy cocky-cool car spins out of control and smashes headfirst into a streetlight my head banging the windshield as I held Cindy back grabbing a handful of breasts, fuck man, steam came out of the engine restaurant workers out front looking on, Joe immediately takes charge telling us to walk away and slowly drives the car into the restaurant parking lot then gets out and tells the onlookers it's his parent's car as he calmly walks towards us and we turn the corner and fucking bolt as fast as we can to the train tracks collapse to the ground and regroup…

Judy bawling her eyes out and I'm holding her close and everyone else stunned but Max quickly coming up with an idea,

"Look, I'll talk to Lori (the owner of the car) we'll arrange something and say the car was stolen man, nothing can attach this to us…"

"What about those restaurant guys?" Says Judy,

"Fuck that" Says Ibby "They saw some teenagers, that's all…it'll work…good thinking Max…hey Zigg, you're bleeding" He taps his nose,

I put my hand to my nose and feel the blood seeping down, okay baby,

"Look, Max see what you can do…let's just split for now man…keep in close touch…"

"No, Ziggy, don't go yet.." Says Judy,

"It's alright, Max will take you home, straighten out before you get there, alright?"

Cindy smiles at me and rubs my arm and they move on, me and Joe walking that all-familiar dreary train track blues…

14.

God only knows why but I decided to tell Judy about my infidelity, well about one of them, the one I lost my virginity to and the only one that was of special importance, here's the story of Ziggy and Nancy crazy babies, the tragic unweaving of that special lap dance dark corner blow jobs and early morning whiskey buzzes, here we go…

There was this particular house that Nazzie, Joe and myself used to pass by every day on our way home from school, small place front yard a triangle patch of yellow grass, shitty brown paint and worn down fence used to see curtains open and close all the time briefly wondering what the hell, one day, at the beginning of a three week out-of-town trip for Judy, there were two girls sitting on the front steps, one a somewhat tall brunette long hair all one length jean-shorts bare feet toes painted red very very pretty, the other was a blond long curly hair a bit bigger than her friend, not quite as pretty but alright,

"Hi" said the brunette,

"Hey" said Nazzie,

"Come here" smiled the blond,

And we sauntered over all cool-like but really looking and feeling awkward as hell, immediately, and I mean within seconds, the attraction between the brunette and me was obvious,

"I'm Nancy" She said, extending her hand,

"Ziggy…" Shaking her hand,

Goddamn she had beautiful white teeth a bit of an overbite which made her pouty lips sit there like a rosebud beckoning to be opened, deep green eyes and a buxom body with curves going in all directions and most importantly she had those very long kinda chubby thighs with just the right amount of extra flesh tanned and powerful,

"We see you guys walk by every day….thought we'd meet ya today" Said the blond "I'm Michelle…"

And we continued into smooth conversation Nancy and myself focusing on each other Nazzie and Joe fucking around with Michelle making her laugh and giggle and blush, she was a good gal, turns out they were childhood friends the house being Michelle's and Nancy visiting from Minneapolis and Michelle's mom was gone for the entire summer leaving the two girls alone, whoa, and Nancy telling me this with her rosebud mouth opening and closing glimpses of her tongue black hair shining in the sun like velvet man oh man I had never experienced an immediate attraction such as this before I was trapped and helpless trying to act cool and aloof and failing miserably, we talked for a bit longer and made plans to all get together on Friday night, what an interesting turn of events baby, what the fuck…

Friday night came and we all got together at Michelle's place thinking we had found heaven two single chicks alone in a house

for the entire summer, man oh man Dixie chicks rub me slightly we hung out and got high and the hours went by and slowly the booze hit us and I puked a few times feeling woozy but rock and roll ready few bennies down my throat and everything jah baby, I turned down the acid that night cuz I wanted to be close to Nancy and LSD and sex/love just doesn't work, not for me anyway, but some of the boys were tripping out Joe was laughing his guts out but looking tense and Michelle had some biker friends there wearing leather vests big fucking beards large motherfuckers seemingly friendly but the rage just barely under the surface, just barely, these guys sat at a table and drank one beer after the other until the there was nothing but a swarm of empty bottles and these tough-ass fuckers patting their guts and hitting on the young chicks and at some point there must have been a couple hundred people in and out of that house, Nancy in tight jeans cruising the place but never too far from me always smiling and touching and rubbing Ross there hitting on Michelle and Nazzie single and sad/happy as always, Joe and Brenda and Cindy and Max, and Cindy looking interesting and pouty and complicated and Joe seemingly relaxed but the LSD keeping close watch and you could feel it and see it man, but there were lots of people from our school hanging out all those peripheral cool kats that you dug but knew you would never hang out with, Nancy took my hand and led me to a dark corner and her tongue came out we were bashing teeth as the frenzied bottom-feed continued, I had her tits in my

hands and her fingers kneading my cock inside my jeans, rubbing and grinding and soft caresses in the smoke filled catastrophe, soft whispers making all the sense in the world, angry silence telling me lies, deceitful young woman ugly and beautiful and goddamn avoidable, I could see Max playing with this young girl's tits from the corner of my eye trying to get her to take her top off, Nancy pulled me in close her lips on my neck then on my cheek hands rubbing my jeans we're grinding and sticking she takes my hand leads me to a bedroom I see Michelle waving at us winking we're in bed her underwear is off I feel her bush in my hand pulsing and throbbing I've got my cock in my other hand trying to stick it in but it ain't working, friggin' hell, I'm pushing and swaying and rubbing and she's moaning and I'm getting soft, well well well,

"It's okay" She smiles,

"Yeah, fuck it, let's go party our ass off"

And we did…

Next day late afternoon we were there helping with the clean-up, just me, Joe, Ibby, Max and Ross, nothing broken just shit piled high everywhere and we sipped on Rye very slowly our hangovers in high gear laughing all the way to the prize in the sky, Nancy coming around rubbing me gently soft smile I felt all fucking warm inside man, whenever she was beside me I felt the heat from her bare arms on mine, soft skin teasing up against my lost-cause-lovely flashes of Judy in my mind making me sad

and guilty suddenly hit by the realization you could love two people at once, and that it causes nothing but shit-feelings in the end but the ride is sweet juicy and unavoidable, whoa, we were done…kicking back on the couch Michelle and Nancy sitting back in shorts Nancy with her golden tan, Michelle's legs milky white and beautiful both feeling giddy tired drowsy sexy, Nancy moving closer and closer they put Joe Jackson on the stereo "On your radio" and everyone loosens up me and Nancy retreating to the edge of the couch and talking to each other like no one else was in the room I'm telling her all about Judy slight wave of sadness across her face gone quickly, large smile distant and beautiful making me dizzy now she's telling me of her last boyfriend what an asshole he turned out to be, hot-jock shithead with nothing but muscles and money and power, fuck him she said angry and hot as hell, fuck him I say, she moves and gives me a quick jab on the cheek then looks around to make sure no one noticed, I kiss her on the lips a bit longer than I should and pull back she puts her head on my shoulder and we close our eyes and Joe Jackson makes us feel good and lost and separate and angst-ridden and joyous thunder with that goddamn temporary beautiful moment already slipping away…

And it continued like that, we got to some serious partying at Michelle's place every fucking Friday and Saturday night, it became the place to be in the neighborhood, even outside of the neighborhood Michelle's place had become legendary and

everyone, everyone wanted to be there, this went on for three or four weeks man, gigantic is what it was, a social gathering of enormous importance in our small and wasted lives and Nancy and myself getting closer and closer and the day coming when Judy would be back suddenly we were feeling kinda sad knowing that this thing was going to end, no temporary separation but a final and resolute ending, damn baby, damn, Nancy with watery eyes singing soft songs of surrender and myself holding her tight we move outside train tracks just behind the house we lay in the tall grass on the other side and this time I awkwardly manage to slide it in as she lets out a moan like a whisper and we start doing it to the sounds of the party in the background I'm on top I'm biting her neck her nails clawing my ass and my back and I don't know what the fuck I'm doing in my virgin clumsiness we bang heads, shit ahh sorry baby sorry, she turns me over and mounts me and I lay on my back while she rides and pumps and starts screaming at the top of her lungs, jesus is this what's supposed to happen, fuck man, yes yes, she's jumping three feet high on my cock in and out in and out I stick it back in with my hand we continue continue continue and it ends, it ends, she slumps down on me her breath on my neck exhausted and smiling and kissing me and we lay there for a second just breathing and thinking and feeling…

"So…" She says softly,

"Yeah?"

"When's Judy coming back?"

"...on Thurday..."

"Hmmm, 4 days...."

"Listen, let's go get rip-roaring drunk and high and listen to The Clash and The Ramones and Led Zeppelin and AC/DC, c'mon baby!"

I dragged her up, we put our pants on and joined the party just to discover Ross was in the bedroom with Michelle and Nazzie was talking up this young blond called Karol and Joe and Brenda were partying up with some people I'd never seen before and we joined in and Joe shook my hand and Brenda disapproved but smiled anyway, so long kool-kats, I'm ready for the long cold night and the purple rain misery and the dark big sleep bring it on I say, bring it on...

So Nancy decided to leave early and go back home, we said goodbye on Wednesday morning under a bright early sun and a sky so fucking blue it almost hurt, that Friday we partied at Michelle's again but things went crazy...the tone was angrier, Nancy was gone and Ross had fucked Michelle then disappeared, (fucking guy ha ha ha) leaving her pissed and bitter, the place was packed and everything came to a boil and suddenly we started trashing the place, we went fucking nuts man, smashed in the t.v., kicked in doors, shattered banisters, ripped open the mattresses in every room, threw furniture out the window, and more and more, and Michelle in horror, and

the strangers joining in and laughing we were caught in the frenzy, we were demonized, we were roman candles in the sky burning with rage and all-consuming, everything that we had suffered up to that point in life came out with extreme anger at that precise moment, and Michelle's house, that beautiful haven that we had stumbled into, that generous and absolutely gorgeous experience, Michelle's house, was destroyed...

Maybe it was the shame of what we did to Michelle and Nancy that made me confess these events to Judy, maybe I was a better person than I thought I was, but I told her everything...knowing how sweet and kind and forgiving she was, I expected an understanding of some kind, some lenience due to my confession...the tears came down like a waterfall and she slapped me in the face, twice, then turned her back on me, and I shouted out after her with all the sorries I could muster and she never once looked back and I sat on the curb as she walked further and further out of my life my head in my hands the sadness engulfing me completely....

15.

Goddamn, I was fucked-up over Judy even though I didn't show it and I ran away from home another three times, once sleeping under the stairwells at an apartment by back-alley park, wake up sometime in the morning walk to the 7-11 ask for the time brush the shit out of my hair and walk to the high school see my friends get high spend the day in the park under the sun in the shade go to Joe's place and shower eat a piece of bread and move forward from there…then my father caught me at the 7-11 and that was that…another time I slept in a small park close to my school for four days until Joe showed up with his mom and they took me to their place and fed me and made a clean bed for me and wow man, it was good to have friends…that too ended with an ungraceful return home and the old man screaming his guts out and I'm taking it at first then I explode and the raging thunder continues, hate and love and everything in-between…

It was all coming to a head…I felt it in my bones and I had always trusted my instincts, even though I was too young to actually know that's what I was doing, I trusted them and I went forward almost entirely on feeling, so on a fucking dreary day mid-afternoon sitting under the pavilion at Crescent Park watching the rain come down slowly like it had all the time in the world I came up with a plan…

"Are you fucking crazy?" Said Max,

"Why not?"

"C'mon man, stealing your old man's car, that's taking this rock and roll shit a bit too far…where the fuck you going to go?"

"Fucking Darryl said if I go to Brandon he'll get me a job at his uncle's photography store"

"Brandon? Jesus Zigg, Brandon makes Winnipeg look like New York City!..what the fuck you going to do there?...c'mon man…"

"I'll be back man, just need to get some money and get away from the old man…I can't take it any more, Max, I can't…I think about my mom all the time…"

"So do I…remember in Italy, that villa we lived in?...damn, remember how fucking happy everyone was?....fucking Italy, what a trip…"

"What happened man?…"

"Beats the shit out of me"

"…lots of good times…lots of bad too…"

"…yeah…"

"Are you serious about this shit?"

"Yeah…I'm not afraid man…will you guys stay quiet when the old man comes looking for me, that's the question…"

"I will…and you know I'll be the first he'll come to…the other guys, I don't know…you have to tell them though, know what I mean?...you owe them that much…"

"Why though, why?"

"C'mon man, this is your thing here, you created this…"

"C'mon…"

"I'm not saying you did it on purpose Ziggy, but this whole adventure, this whole gathering, this is all YOU man, in the best sense possible, you can't deny it…I knew these guys before you got back from Italy, it wasn't like this man, not even close…then you got here and BANG, everything exploded, everything went rock and roll crazy, we all owe you something Ziggy, what you've done here, how we've all come together, it's a thing of beauty man, not one of us has felt so close to something before, I don't know what it is about you or what you did, but it's there, ya dig?"

"I suppose…"

"When are you doing it?""Next Friday man, for sure, no bullshit"

"Christ… alright Ziggy, alright…tell the boys tonight I guess…you're coming to the park, aren't you?"

"I don't have any money…or booze or drugs.."

"Who fucking cares man, we'll take care of you, you know that man…see ya tonight…"

And he bolted into the rain jean jacket over his head disappeared from view and I stayed there and stayed there and stayed there the rain going tap tap tap on the pavilion roof my thoughts keeping beat with the forlorn rhythim, my thoughts

seeing Judy smiling on the grass legs spread wide and my lips all over her…

16.

I couldn't believe I was fucking doing it, I couldn't believe it....I had a lunch packed, ten Nutella sandwiches, a handful of crabapples from Nazzie's tree, 12 beers, quarter ounce of grass, 60 bucks Ross had given me and three packs of cigarettes (Du Maurier King Size) I waited nervously for the old man to pass out and relied on his legendary ability to sleep through everything grabbing the keys from the hook in the kitchen making my way to the back yard into the car slowly, quietly, rolled the car out of the parking lot without turning on the engine then hopped in turned it over and I was gone without a hitch…for a second I got an image of my father's face when he finally realized what was happening and felt tremendous sadness, almost overwhelming, wondering how the hell it had come to this, I was daddy's boy as a kid, I was quiet and pensive and smart and for all intents and purposes a good bright kid, a happy kid, happy childhood, what the hell happened? Where did all this raging beauty come from? I felt myself fading as I drove down Pembina Highway sucking up into my mind surrounded by the most crushing loneliness and the car took a beautiful left turn onto the highway and the city lights were left behind as the country darkness engulfed me…

So why Brandon? Had a friend called Darrell who lived there and worked at his uncle's photography shop said he'd get me a

job and a place to crash so I pointed that little white Chevette in the direction of Brandon, a two hour drive west of Winnipeg, and figured it would all work itself out man, but hell I found driving down the Canadian Highways at night intimidating and hard to focus, shit I'd only driven a handful of times, this was fucking nuts, so I gripped the wheel and stayed away from the pot and the booze and decided to find a place to crash continue the trek the following day under the sun and some semblance of sanity, I turned into one side-road after the other just to find dead-ends or never-ending gravel leading into a pitch black night, some creepy shit man, finally found one that lead to a small parking lot surrounded by forest with signs mapping the way to trails and campsites decided that this was as good as it'll get, parked the car and sat on the hood feeling a bit creeped out by all those fucking trees and stars and the sounds of the bush, held on firmly to the baseball bat I'd brought with me and started drinking one beer after another, one joint after another (always had incredible tolerance, right from day one) the night suddenly not so frightening and the outdoor sounds music to my ears but the loneliness of the country had always been too much for me to bear give me the cities of the world with all their squalor and crime and pollution and indifference cuz this country shit annoys me, and the small animal noises reached out to me and the deep deep jungle-night singing death songs in my ear singing badly in unison with the starry reality being anything but blue man, I sat on the hood tipped my head back

inhaling the ultimate long-lost failure finished the beer crawled into the back seat cuddled up to the baseball bat hugging it tight and thought of things gone and things ended and things beginning and for a brief second saw Judy's face saying goodbye but just for a second man, everything fleeting and temporary and the moment you have it it's already gone, sudden flash of waking up to the RCMP staring me in the face made my eyes open wide darting from side to side drawing the bat even closer to me and tensing up realizing there ain't no sleeping tonight…

17.

So got up next morning and started to drive everything seeming clearer and easier, shit, driving ain't so difficult any fucking moron can do it really, on the road again I pushed that Chevette to the limits stopped at a gas station and bought a few chocolate bars, some chips, a coke, sat and had my breakfast, a few Nutella sandwiches, smoked a joint and blasted into the gray afternoon on either side of me thick lines of trees everything green and full and alive and I actually admired this shit it was alright, man I reached top-speed and the car started swerving from side to side cuz I couldn't control it, fuck baby, no one around thank Buddha I managed to pull over to the shoulder and took a deep breath, baby baby please don't go to the boogie-woogie punk dance, caught my bearings and started up again, let's see what's on the radio only AM shit but maybe some 70's oldies would be on, maybe I can catch a good memory from my childhood when my mother used to wash dishes listening to the radio playing all those soft 70's hits, "crocodile rock", "kung-fu fighting", "leroy brown", "seasons in the sun", me sitting on the floor playing with the latest Big Jim doll with the kung-fu grip, whoa, hmmmmmmmmm, "guns of brixton" came on fantastic song me and the boys had partied to many times head started to bop eating up highway, semi passed me going the other way, hello hello, fancy-ass sports car comes around driver young guy thick blond hair blond woman at his

side looks at me and bursts forward leaving a cloud of dust in my windshield, ha ha ha fucking jack-ass, song ends the news comes on and this is what I heard,

"a 16 year old runaway has been reported missing.."

Fuck shit…I slowed the car down…

"after stealing his parent's car he left Winnipeg heading west…"

Motherfuck…car came to a complete stop and I instinctively reached for a joint…

"his body was found naked shot to death in a red Camaro…"

What the fuck…I was on the shoulder watching the cars go by feeling relief and sadness and loss and victory all competing for my attention…sat there stunned for awhile man, lit the joint, thought about it all, then started up again cuz the world doesn't wait for anything the car making funny sounds, my mind thinking funny thoughts, rain slowly hitting the windshield, every car passing me by driven by the ugly the vicious and the unforgiving….

18.

For the life of me I couldn't find Brandon…I was in the near vicinity but being so fucking inexperienced I had no goddamn idea, drove in circles at various entrance points passed many cop cars feeling nervous and fucked-up money running out, gas-tank almost half empty, moved forward and backward then saw a sign that said, BRANDON next exit, fuck me, went into this small town like I'd found heaven man, small shops and malls and houses and very little activity really felt like a suburban Winnipeg neighborhood, had the address for the photo shop so I stopped and re-grouped…in front of a diner watching the middle class white folk walk around with shit in their shorts, not one, not one wondering who the fuck this kid is getting out of a car un-showered smelling like booze and pot and cynical happiness, bought a coke and sat on a bench in front of the diner lit my fourth-last cigarette and looked around, damn those people were ugly middle-aged couples either completely ignoring each other or arguing about something ridiculous I swore then and there I would never end up like that, never, so I made my way back to the car and took off feeling angry and confused followed directions to the photo shop and pulled up right in front of it…man, it was like a vision from god sitting there all lit up waiting for me, just for me, I hurried inside tall blond woman behind counter in a red vest,

"Hi, my name's Ziggy, I'm here to see Darryl…"

"Darryl Burtniak?"

"Yeah"

"Oh he's in Winnipeg for the summer…"

"What?"

"Always spends his summers there…why, I mean what?"

"Shit…never mind"

"Suit yourself kid…now get the fuck out of the store"

I took off started the car and drove off thinking, thinking, saw a small park with a lot of shade ended up sitting under a tree, hmmmmmm, only one thing to do really, just one baby, back to Winnipeg…I had enough gas to just get me there I figured, 5 bucks in my pocket, a few sandwiches, lots of grass and a few beers, hit the road Jack, hit the forlorn easy tracks back home under the setting sun painting everything orange and gray and red and the highway once again stretched out in front swallowing me into the dreary dusk grind-house , whoa…

19.

I'd driven possessed for just over two hours finished the pot the beer and was without sleep for a considerable amount of time (felt like days, was it?), I was bloodshot hungry-mad for an end to all things, sex lies war and death all the time big semi in front of me remembered Nazzie telling me once that if you pull up in back the momentum and sheer energy will drag you along and conserve gas, yeah I thought, why the fuck not, so I slammed the peddle and pulled up bumper to bumper then let the peddle go…and watched the damn thing move away from me then the car swerve out of control as I managed to barely miss the ditch and come to a halt, re-group, breathe in and out and start that fucking thing up again hit the road hard and fast and there it is, WELCOME TO WINNIPEG, hmmmm don't know how that makes me feel, back inside the Winnipeg borders I felt my powers returning, a surge of energy like lightning up my spine I found my way to Pembina Highway making for the large bush that lay at the far south end of the neighborhood, miles and miles of untamed bush and scrub and whatever else is in those places, I made straight for it reached the borders and pointed that broken Chevette right into the heart of it slamming through branches and wood and bush and maybe even small animals and edging around the small trees some as thin as a ruler (just drove the fuck over those) and the front smashed in and I kept going and going smoke billowing from the hood

BANG into a small tree and that was the end of it…I grabbed my bags amidst the smoke and carbon and what smelled like burning wood and started my trek through the bush which was easy shit seeing that I had partied there before and it was thin enough to catch glimpses of Pembina Highway through the dying green so I followed glimpses of familiar neon signs and I walked and walked and walked reached the highway, I tensed up made my way briskly across suddenly noticing the setting sun and feeling exhausted and blue but I found the train tracks man, those blessed visions of pearl, and took a seat…hot summer night not a breeze, not a whistle, everything silent and lonely and beautiful and purposeful and I took my blanket out of my knapsack curled up beside a bush just behind someone's yard about 40 feet from the tracks, I was well-hidden, well enough, I curled up and closed my eyes breathing the night air hearing the sounds feeling the electricity all around me wishing for all things to rotate and spin to the jukebox music blowing my mind to the alley-cat wonderland blowing Dixie in the wild backyard panorama colors in my head went blinding yellow and a song grew out of that fucked-up teenage sound my whiskey-brain in overdrive, your wonder-lust dripping on my chin, outside world spinning softly, and your dangerous silhouette in that dangerous part of my mind…

Just out of the shower at Joe's place clean clothes for the first time in weeks eating a grill cheese sandwich drinking a coke Joe

cutting class early afternoon he's calm and collected as always so I start talking,

"Thanks for keeping quiet man, I owe you guys…"

"Sure thing man…what else could we do?"

"So my old man actually called the cops on me?...fucking guy…"

"The RCMP too from what I understand…he figured you might go out of town…"

"Or maybe someone did rat?"

"You think?"

"Why not? It's just the inner circle we can trust man, the rest of them don't give a shit"

"Maybe you're right…I'm going to the second class Ziggy, leave before 4, then I'll see you at the party tonight…after 7, cool?"

"Sure, see ya there…"

Hmmmmm, so I started phoning everyone I knew inviting them to the party cuz Ziggy's back in town baby, roll the red carpet and blow those goddamn trumpets, my arrogance blinding me to anything and everything 'cept my triumphant return, so I walk down the tracks reach a front street turn the corner huge fucking house hundreds of people in the front yard rock and roll blaring from somewhere inside, what a fucking party man! I get closer, close enough to recognize some faces from the neighborhood, some hot chicks hanging loose in their jean shorts, uh-huh, fucker appeared in the corner of my eye

jumping out of an unmarked car but in full uniform heading straight for me, I look at that fucking nazi and bolt full speed into the neighborhood damn cop on my heels zig-gagging through yards hopping fences dogs barking cop screaming something into his radio then something at my increasing speed as he starts to fall back middle-aged pot-bellied bastard but continuing relentlessly and right then and there, in a moment's notice, I came to a decision…full stop, turned around, faced the cop puffing his way towards me, c'mon ya old prick make it quick, he catches me, the struggle begins, my fists flailing hitting nothing, he grabs me by the hair, I'm spitting on his shoes, he whacks me across the teeth, I let a gob of blood go in his direction, arms around each other like old lovers we're struggling up and down the street, I'm pumped with all the anger and angst that had built up in me for years I was demonized wracked with misery and optimistic fury man felt like I could tear this pig apart man, he tries to bang my head against cop car but I hold firm, we fall against it and roll around, Judy where the fuck are you? Mother? Brother? Hey Ross, you fucker, ha ha ha, what's happening? Max what's groovy man? Another cruiser pulls up and I finally relent scowl on my face knowing damn well the battle was well-fought and I sneered and willingly got in the back seat leaned backwards staring at the cage in front of me and the back of the heads of those motherfuckers who knew nothing of my plight, nothing of my personal struggle and loss, nothing of my philosophy and

world-view, they would never know how I make people laugh and a sing, how I anger and please them, how I wave my hands when I talk, how I smile when confused, how I light a joint with no time left, how I say goodbye and spit on their shoes as the car keeps moving forward relentless and unwilling crescent moon barely visible in the black sky empty streets wet from recent rain we pull into my driveway living room light on house looking horrible and small, alright I said to the cops, let's fucking do it!

He opened the door and quietly sat at the kitchen table cops on either side of me gave me a long look and burst into tears, one hand clenched into a fist, the other on his eyes, and this bull of a man, this man who had been a god to me, this man who (penniless and without resources) had moved his entire family to a foreign country without even speaking the language, this man sobbed like a child for an eternity, and the cops red-faced and feeling the sadness and myself wishing he would have given me a physical beating cuz it would have been a lot easier to handle as water filled the corner of my eyes and I held it in my heart snapping in two with the sudden realization things between me and my father would never, could never, be the same again…

Laugh

loud crazy

mad and

distant

20.

Went to court, got charged with grand theft auto, fined, and was forbidden to get my driver's license until I turned 21 (as opposed to the regular 16) and after that my father's stance weakened he became distant and aloof and we just, plain and simple, stopped talking, stopped interacting entirely me in the basement and he upstairs and even when school began and I got kicked out of Pembina Crest in the first three weeks for fighting (two in the hallway, one in the back alley, final straw I nailed one of those jock types in the mouth right in front of the principal) he just suggested I go to Arthur Leach where my cousin Max went, filed the paperwork and by the time October came around I was in another school with Max at my side…seemed like the hot girls grew on trees in Waverley Heights cuz this school was crawling with them,

"Does Judy still go here?" I asked Max as we walked the hallways,

"She moved to Brandon…"

Damn, is that fucking town going to haunt me forever?

"If I find out who ratted me out I'll fucking kill him man, I swear"

In my absence I had become somewhat of an anti-hero cuz the boys did a good job of spreading my car-jack story to the three adjoining neighborhoods (Fort Garry, Waverley heights, Fort

Richmond), it was odd but they watched me closely as I moved around the school treating me and Max almost with reverence, and as time went on another gang started forming around me and Max which later got integrated with the old one and the times got even wilder, but we're at the initial days of Arthur Leach everything seeming new and fresh and eclectic manic energy, Ibby was there alright baby, Brenda and Cindy looking hot walking those bloody halls, a few childhood friends were there as well Greek brothers Tassos and Pietro, cool guys man all dark and wild and fun-loving scoundrels, I had decided that year I'd keep my grades up just to keep the heat off as I began the next leg of the great adventure, met a short blond thing with tits and ass jutting out from everywhere called Gerri huge blue eyes said to be easy but selective, selectively easy, and had a tough "don't fuck with me" look in her eye, shook my hand and wiggled away then the bell went off and it began…

Arthur Leach was an experiment, the first of its kind in Winnipeg all classes were in one open area with small dividers separating them you could hear the teachers from the other classes with their ridiculous lectures and opinions, supposed to be some kind of progressive way of schooling and integrating students, don't remember exactly, but I thought it was shit and the teachers were shit and their opinions meant nothing to me knowing I could get by with very little work and fool all of them cuz they just weren't that bright man, lunch time we huddled

across the street in a back alley and smoked cigarettes and Tassos offered a joint we sparked up Max introducing me to everyone shaking hands and smiling and feeling so goddamn at home feeling happy and aaaaaaaaaalright, Gerri standing beside me smiling in her ripped up jean jacket looking teenager-tough rough and ready very light blue eye shadow on and was that a hint of lipstick?

At the end of the day I walked out the front door and there sat a four-by-four covered cab all gray and metallic like a great white shark Ross at the wheel grins and shadows I opened the door,

"So you passed motherfucker!"

'No sweat man, ha ha ha, like the wheels?"

"What the fuck man?"

"My old man's old truck, ain't it great?"

Max and Ibby came running out of the school followed by Cindy and Brenda, I hopped in the front with Ibby and Max and the girls got in the cab Tassos in front of the school giving us the finger my math teacher frowning as we pull out slowly, reach the street and hit the road man, everyone smiling and booze-hungry and sex-starved and waiting for the next turn of the fucking wheel, what a trip baby, what an unimaginable gas it all turned out to be, Ross starts dropping everyone off, Cindy and Brenda first, then Ibby, then me and Max at my place and that was it, the coming of cars ushered in a new era, we were mobile now, the whole was city was ours for the taking, and take

it we did…Joe was next to drive, a red and white Pinto with the engine in the back his mother had given him, then came Nazzie with an old black Thunderbird he named The Batmobile, fucking thing was cool man and we drove the shit out of it down at the floodway as we followed Ross 4-wheeling through the pits and craters bopping up and down drunk and high and rock and roll angry and soon Tassos and Pietro were hanging out with us and Ross hooked up with this young woman from Arthur Leach called Pam reddish brown hair cute as hell tall and thin with just the right amount of curves and Cindy broke up with Max causing him to the feel the blues until three weeks later an Italian girl named Stella landed on his lap (I walked in on her giving him a blow-job at a party) and we moved our bush parties to this place behind a bar called Haggar's Rock Club down a hill right up to the river thick bush giving us some camouflage but two or three high rises stood at the top of the hill just past the bar and they occasionally called the cops but not as often as at Cresent Park so things were irie man, Joe and Brenda tight as ever and myself and Brenda and Cindy forming a trio of friendship independent of the rest, whoa, instead of the good times slowing down they had heated up and were riding the wave with smooth grace and loud-luck rock and roll…early October I was sitting behind Haggar's with Cindy and Brenda late afternoon drinking beer and smoking pot when Brenda pulled out a few uppers down our throat they went mouthful of beer large smiles soon running wacko hair standing straight up

on my head prickly feeling all over my body and horny as hell for some reason,

"I know, I know" laughed Brenda,

"They're aphrodisiacs" Laughed Cindy,

"I never heard of beans being aphrodisiacs…"

"I don't think they're beans…"

"I don't give a shit what they are, the feel fucking great" Brenda showing me her tongue unrolling it like a snake,

"Yum, yum" I say,

Cindy winks at me with that beautiful face framed by long straight brown hair bangs cut just above the eyes tips of the hair brushing the eyelids, goddamn she was pretty but what was this? They looked at each other and lunged wrestling me to the ground laughing and tickling and biting and I'm giving it back and we're having a motherfucking ball Brenda pulls back me and Cindy continue looking in each other's eyes and oh no there it is man, there it is, we pause breathing heavy letting go of each other slowly,

"Hey kids, one beer each left, come on" Shouted Brenda from around the corner,

We ran for the spot as I slapped Cindy in the ass and she pointed her finger at me pursing her lips kiss kiss bang bang…

Me and Gerri fucked twice in one night while the party raged just outside the door, but that was the only part of our relationship that was cool the rest of the time it was a struggle

cuz she was a ferocious flirt and that just would not, could not, fly with a personality such as mine so on and on with the bullshit until I told her to fuck off one night and that was that, two weeks later she was hooked up with Nazzie and they seemed to get along better cuz the Nazz was easier than I was, gentler and kinder and easier to push around from the woman perspective, women could never control me they way they controlled most boys, I was unchangeable and some loved me for it, others saw it as a challenge and others simply were turned off by it, not that I wasn't a good guy cuz I was, and I got along with most people beautifully male or female but that independent nature of mine intimidated some making them afraid and resentful, fuck them, who needs them was my motto, and one day "this" girl was going out with Max next day she was with Nazzie next day after that with me then I was with Ross' old squeeze then he with mine until Cindy pointed her eyes in my direction but this time I talk to Max ask him if he has a problem with it and he says FUCK NO ha ha ha, pats Stella on the ass, and Cindy and I become an item things going real well digging each other just fine and smooth and night-time beauty we were at the river in the bush behind Haggars raging fire reaching for the sky twenty or thirty of us howling at the moon across the bank (about 100 metres) another group of teens doing exactly what we were doing sending us cheers from their side, we're hollering at the top of our lungs, chucking beer bottles and cans into the river with complete disregard for everything

cheerfully damning the world and all in it while having the times of our lives, wild-ass Friday night wanderers twisting and turning up-skirt romances in the blinding rock and roll lonely, wander the earth in the primal blues gutter cuz nothing else will do, wander the frozen landscape roll me on my belly baby cuz we got nothing but time man oh man long seconds at the end of the hangman's noose, wander through the Rose of the Rio Grande heart on your sleeve broken-lovely, alcoholic monkey-man he telling me wild stories in the gangster jungle he playing the clarinet and me hypnotized boy-o and the Dukes of Dixieland are in my back pocket baby, and The Stones had just put out a new record called "Tattoo You" universally considered their best in 10 years and it became our soundtrack, along with AC/DC's "Highway to Hell", The Clash's "London Calling", "Led Zeppelin II", "The Best of The Guess Who", The Sex Pistols' "Never Mind the Bullocks", Cheap trick's "Live at Budokan", Kiss' "Alive" and "Rock and Roll Over", and Lou Reed's "Rock and Roll Animal", and The Jesus and Mary Chain's "Psychocandy", I was sitting on a log by the fire listening to a song called Black Limousine from "Tattoo You" when Cindy took a seat beside me and we smiled my arm around her and that was it, saw Max smile approvingly from across the fire I winked and Cindy came in close felt her breath on my cheek singing the words to the song and kissing me lips hot like that damn fire electric jolts shooting through my body,

"Close your eyes and open your mouth…" She said,

"What for?"

"Ahh, aah, you gotta trust me or this is going nowhere"

"Alright"

I felt her fingers in my mouth and a piece of paper on my tongue opened my eyes saw a hit of acid on hers, cheers, I smiled,

"Rock and roll baby"

She smiled back Zeppelin II now blasting into the night and the LSD beginning its trek through our bloodstream, whole lotta love indeed…

21.

So we started seeing each other a lot Cindy and I cutting class early afternoon fucks in my basement stoned and wired and feeling the energy all over around and inside of us, she was a rock and roll girl with great ambitions at the age of 16 already talking about University and being a teacher or a professor this chick was something else alright,

"What about you Ziggy, what do you want to do?"

"Nothing man…"

"Oh c'mon man, you're just being cool…TRYING to be cool"

"…me and Nazzie are going to start a band, you know that"

"No back-up plan?"

"None whatsoever, do or die baby"

"Put on that April Wine record"

She stroked my cock as she said it and pursed her lips, what the hell was I doing with all these hot chicks, what the hell man?

"Which one?" I kissed her,

"The one with the bell at the beginning…you know…are you listening to me?"

"Yeah, yeah, here it comes man…" And the song started and we got into it hot and heavy fast and furious space-truckin' round the stars making a go of nothing at all at the bus-stop in half an hour damn thing pulls up we're on our way to school all smiles and kisses and leg rubbing under the seat my fingers sliding between her thighs her jeans pulsing, whoa, we get off

my shirt is un-tucked and my zipper down she runs for her class I run for mine Tassos watching me walk into the common area tucking my shirt in and Cindy blasting off in the other direction he's all smiles giving me the middle finger, settle in class teacher frowning at me but continuing I turn my head and watch Cindy's round ass settle into a seat in the class across the area, damn fine girl, turn and face the class, open my notebook feeling sad suddenly, feeling stretched out in all directions, lectures from the other classes offensive to my ears, I hear Max from past the divider in the class next to me say something funny, everyone laughing even the teacher, my mind drifting far far away back to when I lived in Italy in a huge villa up on a hill surrounded by the Italian Alps, every morning walk to school downhill on a narrow winding road for a half an hour through the small village brick houses yellow and orange and red and clay shingled roofs making my way past the cemetery, a few soccer fields, then back to the narrow streets in the pleasant shade hugging the walls each time a car or a Vespa came blasting by, past a café old men there drinking wine first thing in the morning playing cards not saying much, then the walk back uphill after school those same old men laughing and arguing and feeling passionate about everything red-faced from the wine spending their last good years exactly how I wished I would, my Italian sojourn, and then the song "Neighbors" from Tattoo You popped into my head and I went on from there…

22.

I started seeing the old man hanging out with a short Filipino woman, saw them at night staring out from the front step into the street, saw them pull up in the car large smiles in the driveway, even overheard the old man having an amorous phone conversation with her from the vent in the basement washroom which was where I did all my eavesdropping, that's why the old fucker had let me be, bigger fish to fry, well good for him I thought got nothing against some happiness going the old man's way, my mother had a boyfriend back in Italy so why the hell not? The question was, where the fuck was MY Yoko Ono? In no time she moved in and her father as well, but my old man, in those ways that could surprise you, put a lock on the basement door so that I would have my privacy, one key to me, one to him, which he said would only be used for the laundry room or for an emergency, cool I said, cool stuff, and that's when it came to me…

Nazzie used to always joke about going into the pot business with me pointing out the house where he knew a small grow-op was happening, always suggested we break in and start selling, and I of course would immediately turn him down especially since the owner of the operation was a maniac called Mike big and fucking brutal with biker connections, but on this day we started talking,

"You've watched the house? You know the movements?" I said,

"For sure man, he's downstairs, the old man's upstairs, I know exactly when we would do it and how"

"What about after we get it? We can't start selling pot in the neighborhood man, that fucking freak will know!"

"Of course man, we hit the other neighborhoods just for the first time, then we actually go to HIM to by the first pound, you see? He sells quantity too, hell, he'd rather sell quantity, get rid of it all at once man, you know?"

"It's brilliant, you crazy fuck-ass, brilliant!"

"We don't take everything, we leave him some to harvest so we can buy it…I have inside information Zigg, a guy that buys from him regularly…know when the next harvest is coming up, everything…so we hit the house a few weeks before harvest, sell all the pot in those two weeks, then we have the money to start…and the cool thing is that it would be
sanctioned buy Mike, we would have his approval, ha
ha ha ha ha…"

"Crazy fucker, ha ha ha!"

'He's the biggest prick on the fucking planet man, he's done a lot of shitty things to a lot of people, I heard he's killed a few people too…"

"Don't tell me that man, don't fucking tell me that"

"Don't worry man, I wouldn't try it if it wasn't safe"

"Yeah right, when the hell have you ever done anything that's SAFE?"

"Okay, relatively safe, leave it to me man, I'll let you know"

"Alright chico, let's go meet the girls"

"Do we have to?"

"Fuck, I don't feel like it either man"

"How's it going with Cindy?"

"Great...but I still don't feel like seeing the chicks now man"

"Same here"

'How's it going with Gerri?"

"Good, but like you said...I'm too stoned man, I'd rather just shoot the shit, you know?"

"She's a pretty hot fucking blonde..."

"Yeah, but women come at a price...and sometimes I don't feel like paying"

"Fuck I hear ya..."

"Hmm..."

Silence...

"Where are we meeting them?" Said Nazzie,

"The 7-11"

"Fuck...ready to go?"

"Let's get this shit over with"

So we got into the Batmobile and headed for the 7-11 under that goddamn prairie sky relentlessly deep blue and relentlessly beautiful thoughts swimming around my head as I look out the window and see this crazy fucker riding his bike up and down

the sidewalks weaving in and out of traffic causing all sorts of shit man, what the hell,

"Is that Ibby?"

"Ibby you crazy fucker, hang on!"

We accosted him and he grabbed on to the side big smile on his face,

"What the hell are you doing man?" I shouted,

"Just trying to make it home, what the..."

Car horns and obscenities hurled our way, Ibby starts to wobble and pulls away,

"FUCK!" He shouts, then starts laughing reaches the curb, waves and makes the "OK" sign as he pulls away,

"What the hell was he on?"

"Maybe those fucking pills you've been passing around...those things are deadly man...got some?"

"No, and a damn good thing, we're dropping acid later, new kind called black medallion, supposed to be pretty good shit...FUCK ME!!!" He shouts out the window,

"...crazy shit..." Under my breath,

Pull into the 7-11 and there are the girls looking right stoned out of their minds huge smiles tight jeans bell bottoms Cindy wearing John Lennon shades smoking a cigarette and Gerri short and blond and hot and tough jean jacket rocker chick even had a bit of lipstick on whoa, man she alive and willing and Cindy's hot to rock all night long we are a couple of damn lucky boys into the car we all go that long black cool thing easing its

way down the highway to Haggar's then the beer vendor then park the car and straight down the hill Joe, Max, Ross about 15 other people all there as I notice a beautiful black girl sitting on a log by the fire looking shy and demure and just a little wasted it begins again and again we go willing into the deep dark night let the shit fly where it will…

23.

There were also nights when we simply sat at the 7-11 the entire time with the occasional trip to back-alley-park to mix our liquor in plastic cups Rye and Coke man sitting at the corner store watching all the shit go by, leaning up against our cars, laying on the hood, making out with the girls and smoking cigs in the dark, marijuana always there and the constant stream of traffic pulling in and out of the 7-11, all sorts of strange faces getting out of strange cars and fucked-up looking middle-aged women all wasted and plastered with the sad-grin melancholy sunshine, the middle class/suburbanite type there as well with their hot-shit cars and fat wallets and pretty hair and nice sweaters they were the enemy man, not that I wished anyone any harm (not my style) but we did pull some shit on them, our Italian friend Salvatore had a pair of goats eyes, real goats eyes, from his uncle's farm that he dropped in the front seat of a respectable couple's car once as they went into the store, we turned the corner heard them both cursing, the girl screamed and we stood there just a few feet away smiling and taunting the fucker with those goddamn eyeballs in his hand looking angry at first, then taking a look at our leather jacket long hair madness and backing off immediately, another time I was so drunk I grabbed a woman's ass right in front of her pretty blond boyfriend and scowled at him as he took off with his girl in tow, but most of the time we kicked back hanging

around our cars just to the right of the parking lot so as not to block traffic and not get the cops involved, and for the most part they left us alone or even enjoyed us being there you know, the bad boys of the neighborhood with all their color and guts and attitude and their hot young chicks looking cool-laid-back man, what a trip, so on this particular night there weren't many of us, Ross and Pam, Nazzie and Karol, Joe and Debra, Max and Stella, Me and Cindy, bodybuilding Harry and Salvatore and some other punk from the neighborhood tall black kid with a Mohawk called Michael good guy loud and crazy punk-rocker gentle soul, halfway through an acid trip freaking out at all the cars and headlights and funky looking people our beer in the trunks and my Rye and Coke in my cup out of the fucking blue comes this very tall lady in tight tight black jeans big thighs bare feet (in late October) gigantic tits hair red and curly so damn huge it reached her shoulders on either side and around her neck was a snake about 3 feet long just kind of hanging there, what the hell says Ross, she comes right up to us and starts talking and laughing obviously wired and tripped-up on something,

Ross: What the hell is a snake –

Snake-girl: -doing around my neck?....he's my pet, ain't he wonderful? (slurring the end of "wonderful" just a touch)

Cindy: Can I touch it? (all acid smiles)

Snake-girl: Yeah baby-doll, go right ahead (blowing smoke upwards into the sky)

I make a sarcastic remark about the whole thing, the gang starts laughing,

Cindy: Are you done? Are you finished? (looking back at me)

Me: Peace and love sister…

Few more soft chuckles in the background,

Cindy: Holy shit man (petting that fucking thing on the head) this feels fucking wild man (damn thing sliding its tongue in and out) hey Ziggy –

Me: Not a fucking chance baby…

Snake-girl looking at me grimly then suddenly smiling and winking and swaying gently side to side,

Cindy: What the hell is it…wow…

Snake-girl: Python…just a baby…(swaying swaying eyes peering out of that mushroom-cloud hair)

I make another sarcastic remark about the whole thing,

Cindy: Funniest guy alive, isn't he? (to snake-girl)

Snake-girl: I'd like to sit on him all night long, how about you, baby-doll?

Cindy: I just might…how big does this thing grow?

Snake-girl: Ten feet….maybe more…maybe I'll sit on YOU, whiskey-lips…(more swaying and smoke billowing out of her mouth….snake suddenly lurches forward then recoils…Cindy jumps three feet in the fucking air man and runs back to us screaming her head off,

Snake-girl: Shit, so sorry man, I have to go, he's usually friendly, really…(genuinely apologetic…then suddenly turning

maniacal) I have to run shitheads, see ya ya crazy fuckers, ha ha ha ha ha (running into store),

What the fuck I said, we started laughing but feeling freaky electricity around the edges Cindy weak smile on her face legs a bit wobbly that accursed snake-image stuck in my head and Max going on a bad trip saying all sorts of bizarre cryptic things talking him through it the whole time freaking out myself trying to keep it together memory of that night like a collection of snapshots, Cindy crying under a tree, Max screaming about the futility of things, Ross angrily trying his hardest to have a good time, Snake-girl swaying slightly in the wind lights and traffic and sound all behind her, Stella panicking cuz Max is losing it, Harry standing in the moonlight biceps bulging as he downs a beer, Salvatore leaving early looking sad and lonely even as he laughs, whoa, strange trip indeed, strange trip under the spell of the Snake-girl says the high traffic hoodoo guru heavyweight acid-trip lonely…

Saturday afternoon walking the Fort Garry sidewalks with Nazzie hands in our pockets our breath coming out in clouds but goddamn beautiful weather nice and cool and clean many people moving around comfortably neighborhood felt alive and kicking and Nazzie talking up a storm golden leaves on the ground gray sky hanging low,

"- no, no, y'see, that's why Ted Nugent is a better guitar player than Jimmy Page man, look, Zeppelin is an illusion, they're really not that good -"

"Yeah, right, you're crazy"

"Lately I've been getting into all this underground stuff man – "

"How?"

"Gerri's older brother listens to this weird fucking radio station late at night, we can hear it from her room, so one day I asked him what it was all about…it's all this punk shit that's really wild and creative man, bands like The Clash…"

"…I love The Clash, and they ain't underground, they're fucking huge"

"Yeah, but they're not that arena shit, you know?...they're from a different musical background, a different vibe all-together man"

"I hear ya man, bring some over"

"For sure, you know, The Rezillos, The Electric Chairs…"

"…cool name…"

"Yeah, The Buzzcocks, The Velvet Underground, The Sensational Alex Harvey Band, you'll dig it man, believe me…so listen, we gotta get you a guitar or this fucking thing is going to run away from us"

"Yeah, I know…soon man, don't worry…"

"Would you be willing to cover some of that undergrounds stuff?...along with some classics?"

"For sure man, as long as the bulk of the songs are originals...got lots of ideas"

And we continued in that fashion under the barren trees rust-colored grass, couple of kids race by us, a dog barks in the distance, a mother screams out her son's name, '67 Firebird burns rubber right beside us bolts off in a cloud of smoke, three stoned chicks across the street laughing and singing looking lovely in their tight jeans and striped Adidas runners, Nazzie's wiry eyes looking at me with laughter and sadness at the same time talking all kinds of shit waving his hands driven by the manic early morning beer-buzz bounce in his step worn out fedora pulled tightly around his head, myself all sinew and energy and smoking-gun-happy, chicken joint at the end of my block bursting at the edges argument in the parking lot, Vincent Massey High across the street group of punk rockers on the front steps popping pills hurling insults at the sky, Bob Marley song pops into my head "No Woman, No Cry" as we linger on and on and on cross at the walkway start crawling along Pembina past the small apartment buildings, fast food joints, small parks, angry teenagers and the other kind, car horn rips into our reality there's Ross crazy bastard behind the wheel of the Great White pulls up right beside us halting traffic large smile on his panic-stricken face,

"GET IN MOTHERFUCKERS!" We jumped in the back and the shark took off followed by the complaining car horns and curses, Ross opened the small window in the cab,

"WE LIVE IN AN ARTLESS SOCIETY!" He shouted,

"HALLELUJAH MOTHERFU-!"

Truck swerved to the right and Nazzie flew into me,

"Fucking hell!" He said,

Turns sharply into the 7-11 screeches to a halt right beside it jumps out running towards us hands a few black pills over with strange white markings on them,

"Black Beauties babies, down them, I've got a 24 of beer in the front, we're going to the river"

He runs back to the cab and bolts off I go flying into Nazzie,

"Jesus, fuck!" He says,

So we pulled into Haggar's parking lot made our way down the hill sat by the river surrounded by the stripped-down bush realizing this was the last time there for the season damn brutal winter around the corner flying high talking fast and wild Ross leading the show shooting the shit about Pam things going smoothly and wild and he's getting a few on the side like the rest of us bastards man, then and there we decided to include Ross in our marijuana heist cuz we needed a lookout, that's all he asked, that's all man, he was in immediately, and the next day Ibby was recruited just cuz we dug Ibby and it was understood that this was a Nazzie/Ziggy operation and that they'd be paid off in free grass but the bulk of it was ours and we were prepared to take the major risks, alright they said kool-kat baby, so the night in question was upon us…

The house seemed silent up on a small hill with just enough cover from the road and somewhat secluded from the neighbors so Ross parked on the street at a cool distance idea being if a car approaches honk the fucking horn, myself and Nazzie hovered around the back Ibby leisurely hung around the front, everything looked cool and quiet and there was a thin layer of fog in the night with the rain just hanging in the air you could taste it on your lips, expensive part of town huge houses far enough apart to keep things quiet residents asleep early in their fucked-up illusionary lives this should be a cinch I was thinking,

"Nazzie" I whispered "you sure no one's home man?"

"Well we're going to find out..."

"Fuck man"

"Just kidding kool-kat, let's knock on the door a few times"

"Man, if this doesn't work, you're a dead man"

"Don't worry baby, got my mojo working...wait here"

Damn, I kneeled behind a bush and watched him coolly walk up to the back door give it a few knocks, wait, a few more, wait wait and wait...he gives me the thumbs up and walks around the front and as I watch him I realize for the first time how big that fucking house is he knocks on the front door so loud I nearly jump out of my skin that vicious bastard, I see Ibby jump from across the street as well then Nazzie comes walking up slowly and crouches down beside me,

"Now we wait for awhile"

"How fucking long?"

"Twenty minutes or so, here let's smoke a joint…"

"No thanks, wanna be clear-headed for this"

He lights it up takes a puff,

"Here, pass it over" I say,

Ibby comes running up to us,

"What the fuck's going on?"

"We're waiting"

"Was anyone going to tell me?...here, pass me that…"

And there we huddled passing that joint back and forth brilliant red ember like a beacon in the fog Ross pulling up slowly beside us lights out talking low from the car,

"…what the hell…"

Nazzie waving him away angrily Ross arguing back quietly then finally pulling away and back to his position,

"Let's go" Said Nazzie

"Everyone got their bags?" I said,

We move in slowly through the fence into the back garbage bags in our hands basement window beckoning us Ibby approaches and kicks it in crash just loud enough to make us take cover, we lay in the grass for a few long minutes to see if anyone heard us then continue…we argue about who should crawl in Nazzie and I telling Ibby he was the smallest he should do it, fuck you guys he's saying but eventually starts going in,

"…assholes…" He says as he slides down into the house followed by a loud crash,

"…fuck…" He says,

"...shut the fuck up man, c'mon..." Says Nazzie,

"...there's a fucking table here with fucking splinters, motherfuck..." He makes a waving motion with his hand and we run quietly to the back door as it opens and in we go in, huge damn house man took us awhile to find the basement but when we did, when we turned that corner and flashed our lights around it our jaws dropped...that basement was at least 50 feet long and from wall to wall were marijuana plants and apparatus and lights and all that junk, some plants up to three feet tall or more, jesus man oh man, so we started with the ripping and clawing almost in a frenzy filling up our bags stomping it in and filling some more and in our madness tipping over a light breaking it and suddenly getting the urge the blind fury all-encompassing just like at Michelle's house we proceeded to trash the place caving in televisions and smashing lamps and tearing curtains the whole nine yards but just the upstairs cuz we didn't want the remainder of the grass fucked with laughing like rabid dogs we finished the job and got the fuck out of there running down the street with three garbage bags full of marijuana each buds and leaves sticking out of the tops Nazzie's fedora flying off his head took both of us to restrain him from going after it made it to Ross and the Great White and that fucker was passed out at the wheel we jumped in slamming doors swearing our heads off Ross lurched awake with that horror-look on his face,

"MOVE IT FUCKHEAD!" Screamed Ibby,

We bolted out of there man all wired and taut and frenzied energy but within ten minutes driving down Pembina Highway we were laughing and sticking our faces in the green green grass and complimenting each other on a job well done and the world kinda tilted to one side and the sky turned crimson red then blue and purple as the sun reared its head and we paused amidst the vanishing fog and the hopeless teenage victories…

24.

We kept it quiet and dried the shit out even going so far as using a microwave to speed the process and one day Cindy comes walking down into my basement tight daisy dukes white ankle socks blue Adidas red tank top looking so damn lovely and tasty and sweet and tough with her leather wristband and cigarette dangling from her lips all cocky and sure long brown hair falling way past her shoulders and her eyes hazelnut and fucking huge me and Nazzie with a mound, literally, of marijuana on the coffee table, three pounds worth, and we're cutting it in quarter ounces placing it in sandwich baggies her jaw drops for a second then she starts laughing and the questions fly and of course our bullshit is well-prepared, Nazzie fronted it from a cousin who lives in Brandon we have two weeks to sell it all and on and on, she sits down beside me,

"Let's smoke some" She's beaming,

"You hear that Nazz, ain't she cute?"

"You finished? You done?" She says sarcastically,

"Here, light it up"

"Hey, Cindy, you get some free stuff right off the bat sister"

"Huh, I better, no, just kidding ha ha ha"

"You better be sister moon" I start laughing along with Nazzie,

"Yeah? You're funny, believe me…you done? All finished?"

"…I suppose so…crazy chick (under my breath)…"

"So, geez, that's a lot of fucking weed…"

"We've got some sales set up in Fort Rouge and Waverley Heights, some downtown too…"

"I hear that downtown is some pretty tough-ass shit"

"No problem" Says Nazzie,

"Oh I forgot, tough guys" Sarcastic Cindy,

"Okay, put that shit away and let's get out of here Zigg" Says Nazzie "let's make some sales"

"You coming?" Me to Cindy,

"Let's rock Sigmund"

"Alright Betty Boop"

I locked up the weed in a strongbox then locked it in my room of which I had the only key then we were off, out in the car stoned as hell my old man's girlfriend's father sat on the front step in a lawn- chair smoking cigarettes looking out at the world and somehow we found this humorous couldn't stop laughing man trying to start Nazzie's car trying not to look directly at the old man climbing all over each other Cindy's bubble-butt sticking in my face then Nazzie starting up the Batmobile and we were off…it was easy from there, we knew so many people, so many pot smokers scattered across the four neighborhoods and the downtown area (where we kept our mouths shut cuz those boys were really tough-ass not like our pretend-tough-ass one guy showing metal in his jacket pocket, another packing heat, shit hell, we were out of there quick) so the pot was gone in a few weeks, then we approached Mike (that fucker we stole

from) listened as he sat and talked about the theft and how the people involved were dead meat and he was raging mad foaming at the mouth spittle gathering in the corners gorilla body moving back and forth bought two pounds of grass from him asking if he minded us entering the biz in "his" neighborhood "not at all boys, I do quantity, you kids can take care of the small shit, now get the fuck out of here", so that night we got drunk at my place while the old man hung out upstairs in his world and after Nazzie took off Cindy started crawling all over me tongue down my throat I'm on my back she straddles me and I slide in, slip out, clumsily penetrate with the help of my hand and from then on in it was smooth sailing as she rotated and grinded and I laid there making funny noises and she bit my neck and punched me in the gut and I laid back and strapped myself in for the ride as her cum streaked down my cock and I shot it in her…

25.

We moved the first two pounds in one week-end selling the shit at Vincent Massey High which coincidentally had a cop station right across the street, I'm talking 50 feet from the front door, me and Nazzie conducting business right in front of the cop's noses, how did they not see this? Did they even give a fuck? So right there in front of the school and the cops baggies in our socks and in our jackets money exchanged hands and we became the kings of the neighborhood everyone coming to us, even our enemies, cuz we had the good shit and the good prices and were ready to deliver right to the school's front doorstep, and Ross fronting continually racking up a bill and us not caring cuz it was Ross man, Ross, the Greek brothers became good customers and good pals and Joe and Ibby became inseparable with Brenda in tow me and Cindy starting to fight Nazzie and Gerri doing alright Ross and Pam cool runnings and of course there were always other girls, we were always fucking around sharing the same chicks, one week Max had her, the next I did, one night Max, Tassos and myself fucked a girl called Tanis one after the other, don't remember who went first but it was peachy man, then one night I went into a jealous rage with Cindy and she walked and I was cocky as usual pretending not to give a fuck but hurting inside (as always) and another winter passed with us huddling in -30 temperatures and trashing almost every house we got invited to as the old man got married

to the Filipino woman in Hawaii leaving me alone for two weeks had one long party nothing broken all cool Cindy and I getting back together then breaking up a month later then back together two months after that, and winter ended, and the green started to come back as the air warmed up and our smiles grew wider and I got kicked out of Arthur Leach for cutting classes but finished the school year at Vincent Massey High with flying colors, and at the end of May we started hanging out at cottages, Ross' parents owned one, so did Joe's, a few others, our country partying in full swing as things started to move in another direction…

26.

Falcon Lake was about a two and a half hour drive East of Winnipeg close to the Ontario border from what I remember beautiful scenery man thick green trees everywhere colors like fire, gold, amber, deep red, gray, Manitoba forest racing by until you reached the Canadian Shield with those overwhelming gigantic rocks jutting out of the side of the road almost silver in appearance doing wonders to my acid trip, we had Iggy and the Stooges on the stereo, me, Cindy and Ibby in the back, Joe and Brenda in the front following the Batmobile Nazzie at the wheel, Ross, Pam, Max (no Stella), Gerri, Karol and Tassos there as well, reached the cabin late afternoon drove into the winding gravel right up to an averaged size blue bungalow cool man, our digs for the week-end, Ross's parents place, half of us on acid, trunks full of beer and hotdogs and burgers and Vodka and Rye and Coke and more acid few prescription bottles full of various pills, uppers, downers, valium, whoa man, first time for me in the Canadian countryside (had been to the Italian alps many times) so I just followed the lead, seemed like those not on acid started doing all those outdoor things that people do, canoeing, water-skiing, swimming, hiking, shit I couldn't relate even if I would have been straight, so me and the acid-heads (Nazzie, Brenda, Max, Ibby and Tassos) sat in the main room drinking beer smoking one joint after the other downing the occasional pill occasional walk around the cabin through some thick trees

and interesting hilly landscape then right back to our positions on the floor in a circle listening to the new AC/DC album with the new singer (Bon Scott had died a year earlier to our collective sadness) and really grooving with it amazed at how they could have replaced such a unique voice as Bon Scott's, wow baby, fuck yeah, we partied and laughed and sang and played air guitar soon the rest of the gang there too and no one ate that night as the partying continued until the sun came up, and a bit more…

Next day hungover and sleep-deprived me and Ross sat in the middle of the lake fishing eating raw hotdogs drinking warm beer Cindy and Brenda sitting on Ross' dock in their bikinis (red for Cindy, black for Brenda) dangling their feet over the edge waving at us smiling and smoking a joint, the dock went from the back door of the cabin down a set of wide wooden stairs right into the lake which was a curling beautiful wave of blue/green sided by a thick forest of green and brown and red and purple and all the animal sounds that go with it, hmmmm great place to visit, went back to the cabin without catching a single fish and lit a bonfire in the gray dusk, Tassos had been hitting on Karol continually with his Greek charm and that large crooked nose that screamed of personality and was finally wearing her down, she was a tall beauty long-leg-madness full of quirks and strange thoughts, Brenda had began to flirt with me some time earlier in private and I guiltily admit reciprocating as

we sat by the fire sipping on beer her feet occasionally rubbing against my leg pretending it was an accident again and again, that smile and wide blue eyes deep black velvet hair, Gerri seemed to only have eyes for Nazzie and that was a good thing cuz The Nazz deserved it as they sat on the other side of the fire Gerri on his lap laughing and singing popping pills wild rock and roll chick The Sex Pistols blasting out of the back door into the shock-rattled countryside, Ibby was everywhere and everyone loved him a smart Trinidadian kid with a healthy laughter and a good heart you trusted him the moment you met him man Joe never too far from his side, Max seeming rowdy touch of anger in his voice but he kool-kat-Charlie a good time being paramount to him, Cindy continually moving away from me every time I approached her something nasty going on between us man, so I stopped approaching her all together until drunk enough and angry enough I exploded in the middle of the night in front of everyone and she gave it back to me of course Max trying to calm me down Brenda in there too, Joe grabbing my arm as Karol stepped in front of Cindy blocking her approach, ugly scene man, things winding down, everyone retreating to their respective rooms or corners, I went outside sat by the fading fire drank beer feeling lousy man lousy empty war all but lost in the matinee monster movie, Tassos approached beer in hand sympathetic smile on his face,

"Can I sit down man?"

I smiled,

"Well Zigg…that was quite the scene…"

"…how's it going with Karol?"

"It's a done deal"

"You know she cheats on her boyfriends all the time, right?"

"Who said anything about boyfriend? Just want to fuck her"

He laughed

"I find that a very unattractive feature in a woman"

"What's that?"

"Infidelity"

"Is that what that scene was about? Did Cindy cheat on you?"

"No, no, she wouldn't do that…but there's someone else in her head…"

"What makes you say that?"

"Here…wanna smoke?"

"Sure"

Gave him a Du Maurier, lit one for myself,

"Did you notice the way she moved away from me whenever I approached her tonight?"

"The whole room noticed it man, and she wanted it that way"

"She's been doing that on and off for a few weeks now…that usually means they want to break up but haven't found the nerve yet…"

"I think you're right"

"And it also usually means there's another guy in the wings…"

"That sucks man, I know you really dig her"

"Yeah, first Judy...now Cindy...can't seem to hang on to the chicks man, ha ha ha...",

"C'mon man, the chicks are always after you"

"I meant I can't hold on to the ones I want, the ones that mean something....the rest is just fun, it doesn't mean shit..."

"...yeah..."

"...but fuck it man, that's the way it goes"

"...yeah, but you know she's just another chick, right?"

"I guess...yeah..."

"Take it easy man...I'm gonna see what Karol's doing"

"She'll be doing you in no time...if you're man enough"

"And listen, you can do better than Cindy anyway, fuck'er"

"Right..."

And he left, and the next day late afternoon cloudy sky gray horizon we drove back home me and Cindy in the backseat of the Batmobile her head on my shoulder as she slept the entire way, we dropped her off and she got out without saying a word and I turned the other way figuring this particular dance was done, went home, crawled into my place, heard the old man arguing with his wife, smelled food cooking, went down to the basement and reveled in the dimness of that room with the sunlight coming through the blinds in thin slices as the smoke from my cigarette hovered around my head in wafts of blue...

27.

We continued our cabin jaunts quite regularly ending up at Joe's place out by Kenora in the province of Ontario a small red bungalow with a dock just like Ross' going down into the lake and the whole gang was there and things seemed fine until Brenda started throwing one of her fits for reasons unknown took a broom and swept all the beer empties off the table crashing to the floor broken fucking glass everywhere then bolting out the door followed by Joe, man oh man, could hear them screaming their guts out in the back and Ross suddenly started saying in a very loud voice,

"IF THAT WAS MY WOMAN SHE'D BE SPITTING TEETH RIGHT NOW MAN!"

"Easy there Ross, easy.."

"NO FUCK, WHAT THE HELL WAS THAT MAN? WHAT A FUCKING BITCH! WHO PUTS UP WITH THAT SHIT?"

And he continued and continued and continued until Joe came blasting into the room biceps bulging veins on his neck like steel chords,

"WHAT THE FUCK YOU SAYING ROSS, HUH, WHAT THE FUCK? YOU CALLING MY GIRLFRIEND A BITCH?"

"SHE FUCKING IS MAN-"

Joe dove at him all 5'4" into his 6'3" and they went flying out the back door tumbling down the hill and into the dock and squaring off while the rest of us were screaming our lungs out

trying to stop this shit, like a fucking thunderbolt Joe aimed forwards with an uppercut catching Ross right on the nose and sending him flat on his back with blood flowing forth like a fountain, we all panicked, including Joe, and immediately we had him in our arms and indoors on the couch and both Joe and Ross apologizing madly Ross' nose obviously broken, and Brenda and Cindy were crying as was Karol and Max looking forlorn rubbing his temples the rest of us shocked and drunk and high and tired as hell and myself coming to one dramatic conclusion - I'd had enough of the country and the lakes and the woods and the birds and the bears and the green trees and the winding rivers and the campers and the country types with the long ponytails and the folkies strumming their acoustic guitars and the fuckheads in their flip-flops and the hell with the miserably happy lot of them…

28.

The dance continued…

But since Joe laid his hands on Ross things were different, a sacred line had been crossed man and the one person that everyone blamed for this wasn't Joe or Ross - it was Brenda, acting like nothing had happened at all and her eyes roaming from one guy to the next oblivious to Joe who was the most wounded wanting peace above all he and Ibby getting closer the gang sort of splintering still hanging out but in small clusters as opposed to the large group of before, myself staying in the city whenever they went out to the lake fucking the young girls from other neighborhoods partying with strangers and hanging by myself one night found myself at the 7-11 high and drunk when the snake lady appeared out of the mist right beside me,

"Hi"

"Whoa, whoa, keep that fucking thing away from me…yeah, how's it going?"

"Your loss, snakes can be very soothing…it's going alright"

I noticed an accent for the first time, British?

"My brother just got in from Scotland…"

"That's the accent I hear?"

"Yeah, Glasgow, so he just got in, what are you up to tonight? Where's the rest of the boys?"

"They're at the lake"

"Why aren't you with them?

“Don’t like the country, the crickets make me nervous”

“All Along The Waterfront, right?”

“Ahhhh, a film buff, there’s more to you, ain’t there?”

“I could have been a contender, I could have been somebody, ha ha ha…”

“Ha ha ha ha, cool, where’s your brother man?”

She sat beside me, flip-flops, toes painted deep purple, beautiful big thighs in her daisy dukes and tits jutting out tasty-sweet, hair large and wide like a mushroom bomb red curls spiraling down into her eyes,

“He’s in the 7-11, well no, he’s right here, hey Sid, this is…ahh, what’s your name?”

“Ziggy” I extended my hand, he took it,

“Sid”

“Right on brother”

“Listen, we have some Vodka in the bag, want to go down to the river behind Haggars?”

“Does that snake have to come?”

“Ohhhh, I’d love to wrestle you to the ground and trample you, hmmmm…”

“Let’s go”

“Good to meet you Ziggy” Says Sid thick Scottish accent,

“Likewise”

I took off and they followed that fucking snake curling around her neck and shoulders its skin glistening in the damp night

emerald green turquoise exquisite black and red tongue darting out and tasting the bittersweet romance…

On the way to the river we stopped at snake-lady's apartment to drop off that fucking reptile, non-descript high rise right on Pembina where her and Sid and apparently her boyfriend (a small-time professional wrestler) lived and drank and argued and hoped for better and got fucked-up, I waited outside with Sid and we actually got along real well this guy was into all that post-punk music of the time which I had only marginally touched on, I imagined learning from this guy, I imagined spending days in the park under a tree in the shade smoking pot and talking about Scotland and Canada and Italy and man his sister had a set of thighs baby, sis got back looking all smiles and sugar hips banging around singing "it ain't got a thing if it ain't got that swing" waving her arms in the air and shaking her mushroom head from side to side takes me in one arm and Sid in the other and off we marched man, into the night, into the meaningless wonder, into the impending triumph and failure and everything in-between and soon we were by a fire river glistening in the background moon high up scattered teens getting drunk acting stupid things looking strange without the boys, without Cindy and Brenda and Ross and Max and Nazzie and the rest of the flunkies man, but snake-lady and Sid stayed close and howled at the moon and snake-lady told me her name, cool name baby I said, right on she said, nice to meet you

Sheena I said, she winked and handed me a gram of mushrooms raised her beer can and we both downed them along with Sid then she moved on dancing in the firelight with some younger kids life of the party no inhibition whatsoever wild and spun-out-crazy but older than us and it showed in her reasoning as fucked-up as they were sometimes she could get reflective (when she wasn't getting crazy) and those thighs moved in and out like a symphony and Sid exuding intelligence at every turn and by midnight we took off ended up at their place dropped a hit of acid each colors and laughter and madness beginning to seep into the night, damn snake in its glass cage couldn't stop fucking looking at it fucking thing freaked me out and got on my nerves swore that accursed beast stared right back at me, Sheena had Tom Waits in the background something from "Swordfishtrombones" and we were all really grooving Sid showing me his books and his art on the wall, HIS art man, he was a surreal painter bloody gorgeous renditions of Glasgow street life and portraits of people he knew and a series of cubist-type work and on and on and on one of the walls painted over entirely by a mural of a city in decay gray and dank and absolutely beautiful with splashes of red and blue, whoa, man, fucken cool happenings, Sheena had this large book on the coffee table she thumbed through occasionally,

"What's that?" I said,

"The Lord of the Rings"

"Never heard of it"

"Best book ever written...want to borrow it?"

"I just might"

And that was about where the normal conversation ended cuz the drugs started dictating, as they do, and the laughter became uncontrollable slight hallucinations crawling out of the walls right into my fucking lap and the goddamn beer going down like water Sheena gyrating in the middle of the living room Sid rolling his eyes but smiling and admiring his big sister shaking those 24 year old hips to the beat of The Rezillos and The Clash and Echo and the Bunnymen and Joy Division which was Sid's favorite band his short-cropped orange hair and white skin seeming to glow like fire and ice and his big smile hiding an unknowable sadness, like an atomic explosion the front door crashes open in stumbles this large guy holding his ribs and bleeding from the forehead in obvious agony, Sheena and Sid run to him lead him to the couch and Sheena starts administering the damp cloth, the words of encouragement, the bandages, and slowly this guy starts coming out of his stupor grabs a bottle of Vodka from his gym bag and man that fucking liquid went down his throat like ice-water soon he was as wasted as us large large man with fuzzy hair and a healthy brown beard telling us about his wrestling night,

"They carry these fucking pens in their trunks and jab you in the forehead when the ref's not looking, fucking assholes"

"I thought all that stuff was fake.." I said,

"Who the fuck are you to say that shit?"

"Well no, I just thought – "

"- fuck that man"

"Hey, Mark, take it fucking easy" Said Sheena "we're all on acid and shrooms here man, stop fucking around"

"Okay, okay" Starts laughing, "No offense buddy, the t.v. shit is phony but at the small time bullshit level we really fuck each other up" Guzzles Vodka, "But I'll tell you what asshole..."

"Fuck Mark, grow up!" Shouted Sheena,

And that fucker laughed again but I could feel the violence coming off of this guy bad electricity permeating the room and hanging over us like a dark cloud, trying to think of how the hell I could get out of there without this fucker picking a fight with me, which I would not survive, even in my wasted drug-addled mind I knew this, no way I was going to lock horns with this fucking asshole man, he stumbled into the other room holding his ribs leaving us feeling all fucked-up and wired and detached, we sat in the most uncomfortable silence I ever experienced drugs and booze flowing through our veins eyes meeting then darting away Sheena looking angry Sid looking confused myself wanting to scream at the top of my lungs man this deadly silence got me down and low started thinking about the hot-dog stand on that downtown corner beside the old beggar hand extended 16 year old virgin in hot-pants looking mad-bad-dangerous crimson fireball streaking across the sky middle-aged hooker front tooth missing she beckoning my weary ass one I love missing in world-gone-hungry Dixieland trio singing sad songs

amidst angry downtown laughter low-down drug-mood feeding me blue music pornography rattling my brains wrap your lips around me back-alley broken hearts whiskey bottle-shards hitting the off-keys feel that fucked-up saxophone tickling your ribs atom-bomb-luvly feed me sin-soaked dead flowers on my grave warm kisses moonlight smiles on my mind and her distant touch,

her long-dead-musings,

her love-gone-missing,

her hips arching in the afternoon lust-dance,

and your blue velvet beauty grinding away from me in the gutter-love sunlight…

But somehow I managed to get everyone laughing started feeling pretty cool myself until he fucking came into the room again talking all sorts of macho bullshit grabbed that fucking snake and wrapped it around his neck damn thing started coiling tightly his face turning red eyes starting to roll,

"Jesus!" said Sid,

I sat there transfixed mouth wide open was this fucker dying on us?

"Don't fucking move!" Sheena said to the entire room,

"What the fuck!" Said Sid,

"Don't fucking move man, just wait…"

Mark managed to pry the fucking thing loose and throw it against the wall, damn snake coiled and started darting around

the room at an incredible pace, FUCK SHIT SHIT WHOA, I grabbed a lamp and swear I would have killed it without hesitation had it lunged for me, Sheena managed to get it back in the cage and kissed it on the head cooing baby sounds to that devil-beast Mark laughing his fucking head off and then bolting out of the room only to return with a small white mouse in his hand, had it by the tail waving it around,

"Wanna see how this fucking thing eats?"

"Not a fucking chance Mark, no way" I said,

"C'mon man, it's only natural, like you eating a big mac"

"Fuck you buddy"

"What?"

"You heard me"

"Look Mark…" Sid cutting in gently, "No one wants to see a living thing being eaten right now man…I mean, we're on acid, you know?"

"All the better" Said Mark dangling that fucking mouse pretending to eat it himself then moving towards the cage…I still had the lamp in my hand and I tightened my grip around it moving towards him Sheena stepping in front of me,

"Ziggy don't mess with him, please…please…"

"Fuck him Sheena, get out of the way…"

Mark shoves his way through places mouse in cage and everything freezes…we stood motionless in shock as that snake coiled around the mouse and reared its fangs and the mouse

stood there trembling for a moment in eternity then suddenly fell on its side,

"Ha ha ha ha, see, that's what usually happens, fucking mouse had a heart attack, died of fear..."

I gave him the death glare and he smiled back leaning up against the wall deadly smile taunting me and my arm came up so fucking fast I didn't even realize it and down came the lamp over his fucking melon head, glass everywhere, Sheena starts screaming, Sid's jumping up and down, blood pouring out of Mark's skull he's stumbling all over the place I drive him hard in the jaw then a boot to the mouth he falls backward Sheena shoves me aside,

"GET THE FUCK OUT OF HERE, BOTH OF YOU...HURRY BEFORE HE COMES TO, GO!!!

I tell Sheena where I live and get the fuck out with

Sid in tow, we race to my place freaked out in the night tress casting shadows, streetlights with their pale orange orb dogging our every step, sirens always present in the distance convincing us there ain't nothing safe, and we running and running non-stop and shouting all sorts of crazy shit cutting through yards and zig-zagging down the residential streets making for my place flopping on the couch breathing heavy a few beers in our hands trying to shake that fucking experience out of our acid-heads the shivers and that fucking snake and Mark the fuckhead perennially in our internal vision, but even that eventually faded and though we weren't exactly rolling on the

floor with laughter we managed to come out of it and drink beer all night acid trip slowing down, hallucinations diminishing, smoking pot and talking honest straight talk then a knock on the back door and in walks Sheena...

"He probably won't even remember it" She said, "besides he's leaving tomorrow for an extended wrestling tour...and we're done anyway...I don't think he'll be back with us Sid"

"Thank fucking Christ"

"What a fucking asshole" I said,

"Well, he's not so bad when sober" Said Sheena,

"Good riddance to him"

"The snake stays with me"

"Joy..."

"Prick"

And it wasn't long before Sheena stood in the middle of the floor swaying from side to side red eyes all around sun coming through blinds in thin stripes feeling fucked-up and confused and slurring our words and Sid shaking my hand telling me how glad he is we met and Sheena tilting in the early morning-fuck-up like a willow in the breeze we slowly fade away the music melting into a slow lament, the grey moment easing into the big sleep, goodbye yellow brick road with eyes that cry, hello sunshine leather deadly happiness, love song moment bittersweet memory, and the blues always present before and after...

29.

I sat with Max and Stella at back-alley-park middle of the afternoon smoking pot under a tree with that blinding Winnipeg sun at arms reach, Stella she a Sicilian beauty big ass dark skin dark hair fiery and friendly at the same time Max kool-kat easy arm around her talking slowly and lazy and living slow-lovely angst just under the surface cuz things at home lousy old man harassing him at every turn I hand him an eighth, he takes it and smiles, we light another joint and Stella starts talking,

"I can't stand the way Italians eat rabbit"

"How do they do it?" Said Max,

"I mean, I can't stand the fact that they actually eat rabbit"

"Why? Who fucking cares?"

"Rabbits are pets man"

"Yeah, in this part of the world, in Italy maybe they aren't"

"Well we're not in Italy"

"C'mon, if you eat meat you're a carnivore man, why distinguish between animals?"

"Why are you being a smart ass?"

"Gotta be me"

"Eat them all I say, fuck it, burn the house down" I said,

"Typical" Says Stella,

"I'm thinking about that riff in that Alex Harvey song, "Snake Bite", know what I mean?" Says Max,

"Oh yeah, Zal's one of the great guitar players, that's an amazing riff man"

"The way it starts out man, fucking wild"

"I can't stand Alex Harvey" Says Stella,

"Yeah, I guess he's not as good as The Bee Gees, but…"

"Fuck you Max" Says Stella laughing, "and the Bee Gees are good"

"Good for shit" I said,

"Why does everything have to be rock and roll, the boys' way, macho guitar crap…"

"Cuz that's the way it is" Said Max laughing,

"You know, there is good music that you can't air-guitar to, you know?"

"I know jack, baby" Laughing,

"Yeah, that's right, moron"

"Look, there's Cindy and Brenda" I said,

"Notice that Brenda is with Joe less and less?" said Stella,

"Fuck it" said Max "Hey you crazy rock and roll chicks, over here!"

They glide over Cindy in her jean cut-offs hugging

her ass-cheeks and Brenda's terri-cloth shorts crying out to me both with blue adidas runners and stoned eyes that could shake the world man, hellos all around sitting in the grass smoking the grass marijuana in the air continually wherever we were and Cindy that crazy hippie-chick, and Brenda looking tough and rough and hot as fucking hell, alright girls, what you got?

"See, I don't believe that chicks are ever honest with their intentions" I said,

"Watch it man" said Max,

"I find" I continued, "that the more obnoxious and dumb the guy is, as long as he has some kind of status, the more women go for him"

"Oh c'mon" Said Cindy "Talk about generalizations, jeez"

"No really, tell me of one instance where the chick actually, in the fucking end, chose the broke artist over the successful business prick, and I mean in the end, to settle down with?"

"Never" Laughed Max,

"Yeah right, fucking sexists…" Mumbled Brenda,

"I think he may be right" Said Stella,

"THANK YOU!" I screamed,

"Are you done? Finished yet?" Said Cindy,

"So how are things going with the snake-lady?"

Said Brenda hint of mocking,

"Her name's Sheena, and they are going cool-easy…even though we haven't fucked yet"

Cindy rolled her eyes and Brenda followed right after,

"She seems a little weird" Said Stella,

"Now you see" Said Max "Why? What's weird? Why do you guys gotta judge? She's fucking different, so fucking what?"

"She's weird" Said Brenda,

"She's got different ways, she's also from a different country man…"

"Fuck, c'mon, how different is Scotland from Canada?"

"What??? Probably entirely different, a different universe baby, c'mon man..."

"She's weird" Said Cindy,

"That surprises me coming from you" I said "Aren't you the intellectual?"

"I don't like her, don't trust her"

"Hmmmm, interesting baby, interesting..."

"Uh yeah, you're funny, really, wow, inside I'm busting a gut"

"And there she is..."

I was expecting Sheena but hadn't told the gang and she strolled into the park with that large red hair and that awesome height jean shorts tanned big thighs jiggling like heaven forever on your mind and Brenda and Cindy's jealousy obvious and Sheena's 24 year old body shaking her way towards me and winding down into the grass long long kiss her tongue down my throat Brenda rolling her eyes and Cindy looking the other way Max grinning wild-kat-lovely Stella giving Max dirty looks all beautiful and relentless and meaningful and I placed my hand on her thigh felt the flesh between my fingers sun starting to go down mosquitoes buzzing around our heads sound of cars racing down Pembina Highway world passing by at light speed and my head in the grass and Sheena's head on my shoulder limbs wrapped around me like an octopus in my solitude hungry-mind taunting...

Sid had shown up, I sold him a quarter of this new grass that had just entered the neighborhood called Sensimilla, red-hair-sensi in this case and it was ten times more powerful than that Columbian crap we'd always smoked with all those fucking seeds cluttering up the bag, this stuff was seedless (which is what Sensimilla means) and it was Christmas tree green with red hairs running through it, a truly beautiful sight, and we sat in the shade and smoked and blew smoke at the blinding sun watching the world move by easy days at the park and Cindy and Debra beginning to warm up to Sheena cuz this snake-lady had a way about her man, a sinister charm if you will with a razor-sharp wit and an outsider intelligence, she was all there, all there, flaming red curls tumbling down in all directions round face lovely with large blue eyes and a smile that curved up into a sneer she was making us all laugh with her oddball observations and slight Scottish accent, so she brought us to this friend of her's house at the far end of the neighborhood, roguish looking guy oddball outsider kind of small, long arms, thick curly brown hair father passed away used to be a doctor had a cabinet full of pills, uppers, downers, valium, 222's, all sorts of codeine based stuff and this guy had found a way in and gave them out freely to whoever visited (he was a recluse, had pulled out of school long time ago) so we began crushing them into powder and snorting them, 222's, valiums, whatever the hell, and we started buzzing all over the place and getting drowsy seemingly at the same time, for some god-awful reason we

decided to head for the school and watch the summer students do their shit and the whole damn thing becomes a blur at this point, one second we were in this dark, strange basement with wood paneling and an alcoholic mother screaming from upstairs while we snorted pills, the next we were running through the neighborhood with that damn sun high up in the sky, the next we were sitting in the grass at Vincent Massey High watching a parade of students walking in and out of the place, the next I was getting drowsy with Sheena wrapped around me and some vague voices in the background, suddenly I woke up and it was pitch black outside in the thick of the night and I was laying on the front lawn of the school the sound of traffic from the highway barely filtering through to me, lights on in the cop station but everything dead silent, where the hell was everyone? What happened to the gang? Fucking Sheena, that bitch, why would she leave me here alone? How the hell did no one see me passed out, I was twenty feet from the front door for fuck's sake? And those fucking cops, did they ever do anything? Shaking my head I stood up, brushed myself off and headed for home, what a trip man, what a trip, hot night I walked in it without a single breeze for relief everything looking green and full and fresh and silent my footsteps the only sound echoing down the street past the working class slumber and never-ending riot-land…

30.

And it gets bizarre…

When it came down to fucking Sheena, I couldn't get it up, just like that, strange twist of events cuz all I had to do was see a girl in shorts walking down the street and my cock would start pushing at my jeans and Sheena being so goddamn beautiful, what the hell was the problem? Time and time again we tried and time and time again I failed so I would finger-fuck her and we would go down on each other and her smiling and saying the whole time, "don't worry baby, it's alright, who cares" me feeling low-down and angry cuz this just wasn't right man, damn the gods and the horses they rode in on, so I put it out of my head and we continued getting along fine in all other aspects continuing to fuck around without penetration until the whispers started to make their way around and the rumors that Sheena was cheating on me became too frequent to ignore so I confronted her at the river behind Haggars and her eyes filled with water but she didn't deny a thing, not a single word out of her mouth, she moved in closer tears now streaming down her face and hugged me tightly then pulled back and looked at me, kissed me

softly and walked head down out of the bush, into the

street and out of my life….

Things continued in the same fashion but the entire gang was hardly ever there at the same time, either it was Ross and

Nazzie and me, or it was Max and Ibby and Joe, or other combinations of our group but all of us together was becoming rare, the women seemed to bounce back and forth always around in some capacity or another, Cindy, Brenda, Pam, Gerri, Karol, a few others always partied hard with us boys and they added color to our lives not to mention much drama as people broke up and the order of things switched around, Nazzie was now with Karol, Ibby had Gerri's younger sister hanging on his arm, Gerri was single and spreading her legs freely among us and others, Cindy had fucked Nazzie a few times on the sly, Brenda was still with Joe but hovering around the boys horny as hell and the hunger glistening in her eyes, it was an impossible reality to sustain but try we did and the machine kept moving forward and reality kept taking shots at us and landing some nasty blows to the body and head but we rolled with the punches and got off the mat for one more round, one more roll in the hay, one last kiss before midnight, one last joust before the nuclear sunrise, the gods are screaming in rhythm and a horrible music fills the world as our societies sink deeper into mediocrity, art becomes pretension, the masses rule the airwaves, film and literature turn ugly, music becomes monotone, the crystal-white memories of blue-thunder magic passing slowly by raucous sex-talk in your window sunburn alabaster machine-gun ending, all things fade born again whiskey-sour back alley blow-jobs on her knees begging for more, early morning sex-buzz, love fades in the moonlight,

Django plays the strings in the last-call reverie, boom boom and out go the lights, dishpigs run up the bar tab, musicians do the cock-walk ugly as always, that old sweet song on my mind the hours slumber by, with shadows we dance the endless slow-song caress, and the blue-morning dreaming,
and the brutal long-hour sunset,
and the virgin mind-fuck kiss me deadly,
covered in these thoughts I smelled her perfume and saw her across the back alley as she led me in deeper and deeper the tornado in my mind screaming tortured songs unwanted happiness…

And in no fucking time I was in the sack with Cindy again and again we humped in that awkward rhythm, in that no-sense loving, in that midnight ending, and things seemed to look up, the gang started hanging out again Cindy on my arm Joe and Brenda kissing in the corner and Ross and Pam and me laughing and drinking and cursing the goddamn night away that cute Pam red-brown hair twirling in the sun thin long body moving in that reggae soul-movement, I got along well with Pam as peripheral as she was and Ross seemed happy as shit with her man, Brenda winking slyly, Cindy riding me almost nightly jumping high as the moon my cock deep inside of her pills and booze and marijuana swimming inside our heads it seemed for awhile things had reverted back, I almost believed it, until I looked into Brenda's eyes her lips slightly open and glistening in

the moonlight and I knew things could never be the same, never…

My father and I had become virtual strangers living in the same house, he had the upstairs and his new marriage and the screaming and fighting had already begun as I heard them at night while I laid on the bed and smoked cigarettes listening to The Doors, The Stones, The Clash, The Rezillos, The Dammed, The Jam, Led Zeppelin, AC/DC, The Beatles, Joe Cocker, Tommy Bolin, Alex Harvey, Steve Miller, blue smoke rising to the ceiling my mind racing over a variety of memories thinking mostly about Italy and my mother and my brother and how alone I felt with them so damn far away gloomy Sunday indeed…I wanted to get along with the old man, I really did, it wasn't a lack of feeling that separated us, it was a lack of understanding, an inability to stretch our minds and cover the world, so in my loneliness I hung out in that room and listened to the old man and his Filipino wife talk shit and argue about shit then Cindy would knock on my door and we would fuck and get high all night long powder up our noses, smoke in our lungs, her long tender hands around my cock, her sad-face-smile always present, her long brown hair hanging down to her full breasts tickling her nipples, she used to love sitting on my chest backwards pinning my arms with her knees and jacking me off right to the point of ejaculation then stopping just to mount me and ride ride ride till the moment was over, but even this was tainted with some kind of melancholy sunshine, even

this beautiful natural expression of teenage love was riddled with doubt and dark clouds hanging, one hot fucking day we walked down the sweltering Fort Garry sidewalks holding hands and smiling when Ross and Max came running up in a state of panic talking rapid-fire about Sid,

"What the fuck?!" I said,

"He's gone man" Said M,ax

"What?" Said Cindy,

"Last night, behind Haggars, he drank a bottle of vodka and jumped into the river and tried to swim across…he didn't make it…"

"You saw this? You were there?" I said,

"No, we were at a party in Waverley Heights…it's true though man…Joe was there…so was Brenda...he's fucking gone…fuck…" Said Ross,

"…where's Sheena?"

"…don't know…"

I looked at Cindy, her eyes filling up with water…

"Go to her Ziggy.." ,

I took off, made for the bus-stop…

She opened the door in her underwear eyes red and swollen we hugged and stumbled into the apartment as she let out a high pitched scream and crumbled to her knees, I held tight as she howled and cried and slapped me and held me and kissed me and trembled uncontrollably and I heard a fire truck in the

distance and someone laughing down the hall and I saw the sun rise high and proud outside the window and a single sunbeam making an orange circle on the floor and I saw everything that Sheena was, everything that she knew, suddenly fade and turn into dust…

31.

Was at a party in Fort Rouge one night with Brenda can't remember why or how it was just her and me and where the hell the rest of the gang was, but it was just us and a bunch of strangers and I got along with everyone swimmingly which was my wont, small apartment everyone a bit older than us but good rock and roll rowdies, I sat in a chair in the middle of the living room and Brenda sat on the arm, we talked about music and movies and sex and all that other beautifully useless stuff and before I knew it Brenda was on my lap moving her thighs gently over my cock unbeknownst to anyone else but I was feeling it, I was feeling it man, we kissed a few times and it was perfect cuz no one knew us here even though our reputation had proceeded us, everyone had heard of the Fort Garry boys, we were infamous in all the adjoining neighborhoods and these fuckers knew me by name, I acted cool and bashful about the whole thing but was secretly basking in the glory, Brenda was entertaining as usual the guys and girls digging her, she told stories and danced around the room then plopped her ass back on my lap and those thighs started moving again, what a trip baby, what a performance sudden rushes of guilt running up and down my spine,

"We're already broken up Ziggy, neither of us has had the guts to actually tell each other yet, but he knows it…we haven't had sex in ages man…"

"Okay, okay, I don't need to hear that...and that doesn't make this right"

"Since when do you give a shit about what's right?"

"C'mon Brenda, that's unfair man, I don't like to hurt people, you should fucking know that...and what about Cindy, she's your fucking best friend"

"She told me the other day that you guys aren't an actual "couple", that you're free to see other people"

"Really? That's not what she says to me...why are all you chicks so fucked up?"

"I can say the exact same thing about boys...besides, you're supposed be the artist right? The romantic poet? The rock and roll guitar god? I thought you guys lived by your own rules, what did they say in english class? Artists create their own moral universe...something like that..."

"That's pretentious artsy bullshit man..."

"Can I have another beer?"

"Of course...don't even ask, the case is right there"

I watched her ass bounce JUG JUG to the case of beer as she bent over and came right back to my lap

and the bottom of her thighs jiggled and grinded on

my cock, whoa...

"Anyway, we haven't done anything Ziggy, so chill out man"

"So if you're so cool about this, and Cindy is so cool about this, and Joe is so cool about this, why don't we tell them both that we're hot for each other?"

"Cuz the world doesn't work like that, and you know it"

I sold some grass to our hosts and we got the fuck out of there and goddamn it there we were in my room fucking each other silly rolling and twisting and biting and kissing and hair pulling clawing ripping tearing each other to shreds man, we were as hot as it gets after several years of wanting each other and finally getting there, Jesus Marimba we could have been in a porno the way we went at it, holy fuck, she took me by the hair and shoved my face into her pussy wrapping her thighs around my head so damn tight I saw bright lights and heard a cricket playing a violin, a moondance slowly making its way to my upside down vertigo, I was on top going smooth and easy cuz this chick was wearing me out, I move in rhythm to her body, I tongue her face and her small hungry breasts nipples pointing straight up staring me in the eye saying, HELLO MOTHERFUCKER, YOU DONE YET?, and there are times when sex just isn't working, when it's more of a struggle than anything else, when every awkward movement screams with redundancy and you can't wait till it's over, this wasn't one of those times, this was one of those times when Charlie Parker is blowing the horn in the background and your ass has the rhythm down pat, your ass is slow-easy-groovy and nothing you do is wrong everything animal and primal and beautiful, we roll around, I cum inside of her, she moans long and mournful then follows with a few softer short ones, holy fuck indeed...

32.

Following night I was with Cindy walking under the trees and the stars past the residential colorings and sounds and the hot still darkness moon three quarters full we were tipping forwards hopped-up on rye and coke and marijuana music moonshivers few lines of 222's up our noses jerky motions in the green grass sudden mind-fracture,

" - but it's only here, in this part of the world" She said "that we can worry about all these big existential ideas, in other parts of the world they're too busy starving to death"

"It's quite a luxury man, you know?"

"What do you mean?"

"Living in this part of the world…we're damn lucky…"

"Oh, this coming from mister i-hate-society himself?"

"C'mon, that's just rock and roll speak, know what I mean?"

"I know, just teasing" Takes my hand while looking across the street, pauses, turns and kisses me softly as I gently stroke her jeans, hmmmmmmm,

"I always liked how smart you are Ziggy"

"Oh yeah?"

"If you ask any of my ex-boyfriends, ask Max for instance, what does Cindy like in a guy, they'll say down to the last one, she likes smart guys"

"I thought you were a rock and roll chick, party hard till you drop kind of shit…I've seen you with some dopes, ha ha ha ha"

“Yeah, but that was just sex…a stiff cock is always welcome, ha ha ha ah ha”

“That’s quite the mouth chica…”

“Ahhhh, you dig it”

“I do…”

We sat on the grass in the middle of a schoolyard drinking our rye and wrestling around her sitting on my chest with her knees on my arms laughing and bouncing up and down we turn up and over then our lips touch and the heavy petting starts and her buttons come undone I motion over to the hockey rink and the penalty boxes and soon we’re inside and my pants are down to my ankles and her lips are around my cock and we’re moving along as she rolls me on my back and grabs my prick stuffing it deep inside of her and she’s slowly rotating her hips as she moans and sobs and groans and starts to bounce up and down, slowly at first, then picking up momentum jumping high up in the air and landing on my pelvis over and over again and I’m slipping in and out under the cock-torture each time she smiles and lets out a chuckle digging the clumsiness of the whole affair, I slip out, she grins wide and puts me back inside, repeat and repeat and a few sharp pebbles digging into my back and broken beer bottles right beside my fucking head and dirt leaves stuck in Cindy’s hair and the beauty and humor and laughter and sadness and erotic sex-energy down and dirty and teenage-love as my head starts to spin from all the booze and drugs and lost-highway thinking feeling nauseous like the vomit might

come up any second I start hearing the keyboard solo from "Light My Fire" in my head, the whole damn thing note for note, Cindy smiling from ear to ear,
my body goes limp,
I'm inside of her reaching for the sky,
Cindy lets out a sex-howl,
the grinding intensifies…

It continued like that for two weeks Cindy and Brenda alternating nights my groin feeling the sweet-torture-rock and roll, funny thing is how similar they fucked, their movements , their style, even the order in which they did things were almost identical, if I closed my eyes it could have been either of them, it made no difference whatsoever, but when I allowed myself to actually feel it, to go beyond the physical sensation and dig deeper, the two encounters were entirely different experiences, everything is internal all said and done and this bizarre situation opened my eyes and created alleyways in my brain for the electricity to flow through , for the bright shiny lights to show me the way, for the elusive magic to touch me sporadically but deeply, for the white/light white/heat lonely rock and roll burst, AND THIS ONE'S FOR ALL THE WONDER AT THE EDGE OF THE SUICIDE LOVE MACHINE, for the realization that it's all dandelion wine in the stormtrooper barn-burner, for the BANG UP BLOW OUT honey baby you've been good and sweet and elusive sun dance down the long winding

road, and finally, like it always does, the party ended...phone rang I picked it up to Cindy screaming her head off in my ear the most vile insults directed at my manhood and my general character and how could I? and who did I think I was? and I was lousy in bed anyway, and fuck you fuck you damn you to hell then Brenda came on the fuck you's and the go to hell's intensifying, seemed Brenda was somehow forgiven for her role in this affair and it all came down to me, and I listened as Cindy accused me of infidelity over and over and Brenda accused me of being the biggest asshole on the planet and of how lousy I was in the sack (that one coming over and over again) then they went on separate phones and both hurled at me at the same time and I listened and listened and finally shouted at the top of my lungs,

"FUCK YOU!!!"

Dead silence...I could hear them breathing, one of them crying softly, I felt broken but angry and defiant and damn ready to cut them loose the silence and soft crying continuing until I threw the phone against the wall and said good riddance and goodbye to two of the most important people to ever enter my life...we never spoke again...a year and a half later Brenda moved up North to Churchill and got married to a fisherman almost twice her age...two years later she was divorced with two kids and had found Jesus...Cindy stuck around and got a University degree in Psychology...moved to Vancouver, also got married and divorced, no kids...somewhere down the line she

settled in a lesbian relationship with a fashion photographer…that's the last I heard of either of them…

33.

Ran into Joe a week later at a party and the shit hit the fan as it would, I was talking up a storm with some boys from another neighborhood when I felt a push from behind and my beer bottle bash into my teeth, Joe was there and he was pissed fuming pissed zone-red type of anger fists clenched, I knew what had to happen, and as the sadness gripped my heart, as the overwhelming feeling of finiteness sunk in I shoved him into a wall of people, his beer bottle went flying into the air and he froze eyes locked on mine, we paused as the universe paused with us, the look in his eyes pure torture, my betrayal etched into his face in thick red lines, the end of all things imminent, my old friend, do you see? Where did all the late-night carousing and human connections get us? What did the sad-mad-wisdom bring us in the end? The sweet-touch-sugar of her thighs ultimately leading to the hangman's noose always and forever, he tightens up, recoils then lunges forward throwing the first punch landing squarely on my jaw and as the saddest moment in the universe encompasses me completely I hit back and we squared off and the blows started raining on both sides, I landed one by his ear, received a kick in the guts, gave one back, then the gang comes running into the room, Ross, Max, Nazzie, Pam, Karol, Geri, Petros, Tassos, Cindy, Ibby, and Brenda was the first one in, she screamed as loud as she could throwing fists at both of us in the flurry of insanity I see the

looks of disbelief on everyone's face, the look of unavoidable disaster and the long dark bottomless abyss staring right back at us, Max finally throws us apart and we stand there panting and puffing and Joe red-eyed and sad, myself in a state of shock, Brenda and Cindy in background tears streaming down their cheeks, Joe's eyes unwavering from me saying it all, all the questions and disappointment and utter let-down registered painfully on his face for all to see and for the hundredth time my heart broke into a million tiny pieces and the pieces floated in the air like snowflakes hovering above us the last touch of magic in the air as they slowly turned to powder and hit the ground nothing but dust and ash and the end of it all resonating in the deadly silence…

34.

My father out back barbequing with his wife's family sisters brothers nephews grandmothers the old Filipino man sitting in a chair squinting out at the street as he always did one cigarette after the other Jamaican beer in his hand brings a smile to my face my father's wife happily whistling along stomach round and healthy 7 months pregnant ultrasound telling us it's a boy I was going to have a little brother of all unexpected things I watch this from the bathroom window seeing my old man so happy and the small kids running around smell of meat burning on the pit scattered beers on various tables bottles of wine everywhere it was a cool sight man, I felt good for the old boy, he pauses, reflects, then heads for the house, I walk out into the living room hoping to make it downstairs before he enters the house, he calls out my name, asks me if I want to eat something first words spoken in 6 months, no that's alright, you sure, yeah yeah but thanks, he stands there hands in pockets looking down at the floor, I'm staring at the wall, he turns around and walks back into the yard to a group of cheers, I head downstairs make a Capicollo sandwich and pour a glass of water, knock at my door Nazzie comes down the stairs large garbage bag in his hands something long in it small guitar amp in his other hand, he unfurls the package and fuck me, a beautiful flying V Gibson comes out wood panel gold frets guitar chord the whole works,

"What the fuck?" I said,

"It's yours man"

"What?"

"Just what I said baby"

"How the fuck?"

"I stole it, what a fucking blast man…I was walking down Portage by Encore Music, 3 in the morning, flying high on acid pissed and stoned seeing all sorts of colors and things man, streets empty not a car or anyone in sight weird fucking feeling in the air, then I saw it, holy fuck, this fucking guitar in the display window light shining down on it, it looked like a gift from the gods man, and I'm damn sure it was, so I found this huge fucking rock – "

"Jesus fuck!"

"See the nicks here on the side? That's where I pulled it through the broken window, see?"

"Goddamn baby, you're the man!"

"That's what the say man, that's what they say"

"But look, you can sell it, Christ, it's gotta be worth a couple thousand bucks at least"

"No way man, we have to get this band on the road

before we get too old, seeing you play last week at that pasty was inspiration baby, my parents said we can jam in my basement every Saturday afternoon and Thursday night, my cousin plays bass, all we need is a singer, see?"

"That's fucking cool man, that is fucking cool...well thanks buddy, I don't know what to say...let me get you drunk at least..."

"You got it...down by the river behind Haggars?"

"Let's do it"

So in late September, golden leaves all around us, gray sky, barren trees, brisk wind, we wrapped our leather jackets around us and we drank and we smoked and we laughed and we sat in silence and we laughed some more and the sun went down down down Nazzie mentioning how he partied with one of those jock guys we had clashed with over Donna and Shannon and those gals and how he was actually a good guy and a strange memory that one, those straight-laced chicks suddenly thrust into our boozy rock and world and the final fight that ended it all, we had hung out for a year that being the initial version of the gang, Nazzie was there but he wasn't so wired shorter hair, Ross there too, me and Joe just starting to get to know each other, Max by my side as always, and that was it...Donna and Shannon were of a different mold than Cindy and Brenda and that bunch, they were more upper-class, more pristine, more straight-laced, but they weren't snobs by any stretch of the definition, just nice girls that had somehow hitched up with the wild bunch, they loosened up with us, their hair got longer and their jeans tighter, they smoked pot and did other drugs though it was still frowned upon by their peers, they weren't as free sexually as the later girls but weren't nuns either, it was a good

time though I see now that it was just a prelude for things to come, a foreshadowing of the heavenly maelstrom, as they partied with us they also associated with the "popular" boys, the jocks, the older good looking guys with their fancy-ass sports cars and their football trophies and their trendy clothes all laid out by mommy and daddy and fuck it all, this would not have been a problem of course cuz it was easy come easy go but these fuckers had decided to have a PROBLEM with US, they didn't like our long hair, our leather jackets, our taste in music, our drug use, our rock and roll cavalier attitude towards life, and funny thing is that I was friends individually with a few of them, one on one they were alright man, they were just wild-ass kids doing what was expected and what was expected was to rule, right? We had no problem with anyone who didn't harass us but we also weren't shy at retaliating, so these fuckers decided to make us their enemy and the harassing began, long hair fuckers! Drug addicts! Leather jacket losers! The insults were hurled continually, in the halls at school, at parties, in the schoolyard, on street corners, and us giving the fuck yous in chorus unafraid and ready, tension building and building with the girls cuz they were hanging with the enemy, one night we had partied on the outskirts of town at a farm, me, Ross, Max, Joe, young black kid we knew called Micheal punk-rocker wild-ass beautiful, hundreds of people singing late insults into the sky, end of night we drove back to town drunk and high as hell hit a late night burger joint when in comes Nazzie all beat up

and bruised and bloody lip and black eye starting to well up t-shirt ripped around the chest and waist,

"What the fuck?" I said,

"Those fucking jocks man..."

"What?!" Said Ross,

"I was at a jock party with this chick from school, the whole fucking football team was there, everything was cool at first but..."

"Oh fuck man, this is fucked..." Said Joe,

"They fucking started harassing me and took me

down man, laid into me"

"FUCK!" I said,

"That fucking guy, the star football player, what's his name?"

"Derek?" Said Max,

"That big motherfucker?" Said Micheal,

"Him man, that fucking asshole started the whole thing, he fucking laid into me man, fuck"

We jumped into Ross' great white and mad like mad for the party...

Pulled up to the place about twenty or thirty people on front lawn music blasting out of the fucking place new wave bullshit "flock of seagulls" something like that, we pull up on the front lawn I see a hint of fear on Micheal's face, Max jumps out and walks straight up to the first person young innocent looking guy fear on his face,

"Where the fuck is Derek?

"What the hell?"

Tall lanky guy comes out of the house,

"That's one of them man!" Shouts Nazzie,

Makes a straight line for him, the guy puts his fists up, they start moving around but Nazzie fast as hell and angry and us behind him giving him moxie, he lands a kick and a quick right cross fucking guy goes down like a sack, 'nother guy moves towards me I waste no time and crack him one on the side of the head, he pauses, big guy but look in his eye not there, I land another to the neck and a knee to the head, everything is loud and violent and grim forecast on the horizon, the fucking front door explodes and out comes Derek, Jesus man, this guy was the star football player and he was fucking huge, fucking monstrous slow-witted gorilla looking for blood, he's screaming out challenges, we freeze, he grabs Nazzie and starts shaking him around like fucking nothing, we're still in a sort of shock as more and more people start rolling out of that forsaken house and clouds looking dark and unforgiving, but suddenly Max, all 5'4" of him lunges towards Derek, all 6'4" of him, and grabs him around the waist, that large monkey lets go of Nazzie and starts struggling with Max, seems like everyone froze as this went on Max moving from left to right Derek struggling for position maneuvering around him going down left right as Max with incredible strength and purpose flips him over and that fucking ignorant gorilla fuck goes down and Max starts landing blows, I immediately jump in out of the trance and start landing

kicks to Derek's head the rest of the boys in there we lay a beating to the guy people still pouring out of the house the enemy multiplying, Derek passed out we moved back crowd slowly recovering from the initial shock moving towards us, scrapes starting up everywhere, 7 or 8 of us and hundreds of them most just watching but increasingly hostile, Max slugs a guy, Ross pushing off, Micheal swinging back and forth, Joe right beside Max waving his arms covering his flank, me Ross and Nazzie cornered fighting our way out of it one guy trying to hit me with his beer bottle again and again I'm ducking and weaving and landing the occasional shot, big fucker rips Max's shirt, Joe spits on someone's shoes, Ross trips a guy and goes down with him, nothing really happening yet but the foreshadowing horrendous as hundreds of people covered the entire block, lights going on in windows, dogs barking, volume immense and ugly, and us moving slowly but steady towards Ross truck still cocky and fuck you to hell, jock guy that I had smoked pot with from time to time, the enemy, came up to me,

"Ziggy, you guys better go…you're going to get killed man…"

I nodded and smiled and we kept moving back finally made it to the truck hopped in and pulled out, beer bottles hit the side, I got a shot in the ribs as I jumped in the back, Joe kicked some fucker in the head as Max threw another guy over his shoulder, we pulled off and burned rubber man large crowd running after us, that's when I noticed Michael was still there, fuck man, saw him turn towards us but the crowd between us and him was

impossible, so he took off towards the school yard and a huge crowd followed,

"He'll make it man, don't worry!" Shouted Ross,

We got the hell out of there man feeling the wild electricity and the rock and roll respect we had earned, and Michael did make it out of there alright, and those fucking jocks, no word of a lie, never bothered us again, not once, not a word, but Shannon and Donna and those chicks had to choose, and choose they did, we went our separate ways the day after, but I tell ya, I tell ya under the blinding sun of hindsight and optimism, there are times, not often I hope, when violence is the only way…

This strange fucking gray cat black stripes with a huge gut climbing up a tree in front of us obviously stealing its way towards this beautiful canary idling the time away on the tip of a branch fucking cat getting closer and closer I picked up a rock and threw it in its direction scattering both the cat and the canary sun gone moon up,

"You know, my mother and my brother are moving back next month…"

"Oh yeah?"

I nod my head, "I'm moving in with them…not even telling the old man…just grabbing my guitar and getting the fuck out…"

"What part of town?"

"River Heights…'

"Shit, that's really far…we're still going to start the band up, right?"

"Most important thing right now man, you bet we are…so anyway, my uncle found a place for them, big fucking place apparently…"

"Max's dad?"...

"Yeah…her boyfriend's coming with her…he's 17 years younger…"

"Good for your mom…"

"That's what I say…"

Nazzie puts his hand on my shoulder we smile and I say something funny our laughter echoing through the dying bush into the parking lot and down the street…

A SHORT STORY

Goddamn, max's birthday, ross and I decide to take him out for a big one man, place called "the native club" huge minor league hockey arena converted into a social hall five bands playing there tonight so we drop a hit of acid each, pump up the great white and off we go, whoooooooo, racing down pembina highway pedal to the metal passing beers back and forth and the grass filing the car with smoke hurling cheers out the window at all passerby's we groovin' down paradise alley, we smoking in the boys room, we kung-fu fighting at the lonely corral, cop car ahead sudden stop to things...the bastards move on and we let out a shout, a shout of triumph failure and eternal love all wrapped up in that rose colored package with the all-seeing eyes of agamotto, led zeppelin on the radio then a sudden switch to alex harvey then an even more drastic switch to something jazz...a busy bass line...a sax...drummer playing the rim...no no, leave it here man, this is damn fine cooooool easy rhythim, how goes it max my man, my cousin, my lifelong friend, long way from italy ain't it?

what a fucking crowd man, thousands hanging out around the edges looking wired and tough and happy and the bikers are out in full force hogs roaring thunder their chicks all tough baby leather bras biceps bulging crotches wet and ready man, we walk right through them no fear venom smiles acid beginning to take hold, hmmmm, what the hell baby, what the hell, nervous

energy hovering over us like a halo of misguided love, ughhh, harrumph, pay our tickets and jesus christ man, bouncers so damn large bikers looking tiny in comparison arms twice the size of my head not a smile nor a friendly gesture of any kind - intimidation goes a long way in this type of crowd – past those Neanderthals an insane gathering of freaks, painted faces, women with their tits hanging out, everyone in costume of some kind or another and us flying on acid soon we're right in the crowd talking people up charming and humorous and loveable acid freaks, another hit of acid comes our way "black medallion" first type was "orange phonix", wondering what two different types of acid would do to our bodies and mind but fuck it man, let's do it!

max all smiles digging his birthday something fierce first band a hard rocking trio covering zz top, Steppenwolf, ccr, lenard skynird, bikers really digging this shit max out front by the stage grooving with some hot and tempting devil-girl man, she blond and wild and willing, ross and me pumped full of acid and grass and rye and coke, one drink in each hand cigarettes dangling from our lips I'm winking at young girl over to the side, she flips me the bird and I start laughing uncontrollably, ross looking around joins in the color vibration shaking and pulsating and we're busting a gut and shapes and shadows and brilliant red electricity is shooting across the room man, all around me are the pink flamingos they've got vodka martinis and beer bellies and harley davidson t-shirts, max joins us,

what's up baby, what's up, we tell him about the girl he starts laughing rolling on the ground shaking and mooooooooooving uncontrollable and righteous and the parade of freaks continues, girl with glassy eyes in a wonderwoman outfit stands alone biting her nails thighs large and tanned and oh so juicy i'm picturing them wrapped around my head face turning blue yum yum, guy in a zorro mask on the dance floor doing crazy things with his cape, girl with tank top rolled down just enough to show her tits (no bra) running around the place grabs max by the hair and shoves his face into her tits his tounge's out ooooh baby, where did all these freaks come from? did they have other lives outside of this wicked maelstrom of ideas and movement? seems to me they are permanently wrapped in this space in time replaying the night over and over again like a broken record exactly the same down to the most miniscule of details, so how do we get out man? I say this to max and ross and they looked freaked out for a moment but then comes the laughter and the colors and the desperate desperation and that damn multi-colored electricity frying my brain into beautiful crisp enchiladas…

two or three bands have gone on, or was it four, shit don't remember max looking a bit paranoid ross too so i let the jokes fly and i get them laughing again and again and jesus christ the booze is flowing, the freaks are marching, the duel acid attack playing tricks on our minds but we digging it and we digging down deep and our consciousness expanding by the second all

thoughts as one, all ideas nothing but shit in the sand, we did it man, we did it, we get it, we get it blindfold finally lifted, surely these thousands in this damn rotten alive and beautiful place get it as well, they must, fucking monkeys in costume, bouncer checking us out maybe he suspects we're underage, i point it out to ross, hmmmm, max says fuck it, so we say fuck it but we're ready to run man they way i feel i could run at the speed of light baby, warp-drive has nothing on me i'm the flash with two hits of acid for a jet engine and a tank full of rye and coke and grass, ross starts talking to some joes, seems they're on lsd as well, ross is extending his hand, they place something in it, he walks over with two tiny microdots fingers at our mouths, "hmm, I don't know man" says max "yeah, what he says" i add "– plus…" before I could finish ross sticks the microdots in both our mouths and knowing the wastage of drugs as the ultimate sin we chew and swallow, "it's called purple microdot, should be wild" says ross, hmmmmmm, three different hits of acid, let us see shudder runs down my spine and those fucking flamingos breathing down my neck max still smiling band onstage covering "take me to the river" by the talking heads and suddenly all the angst is gone man, suddenly a perfect rock and roll vision makes itself known and ross is on the dance floor with some hot young broad in leather pants and leather mask spilling his drink on himself every time he twists and turns laughing loud and mad and beautiful, max in a circle of freaks downing the liquor tugging on wonderwoman's skirt as she

spins in front of him over and over and up and under, i turn big fucking bouncer still there he holds my glance, winks, smiles, moves away, alright baby, understood…

so the rest of the gang turns up cindy, joe, nazzie, brenda, karol, cindy sees max frolicking with wonderwoman and frowns, "shit" she says to me "I thought he dug me", he does baby, he does, it's just the acid and the booze and all these fucking freaks, she comments on all the costumes and wonders why, I notice joe and brenda snuggling up to each other and ask cindy what the fuck's the fuck, "they got together last night" she says "what do you mean 'got together'?" "they fucked…lost their virginity man, ain't it cool?" I look over at joe and wink, he returns the favor, but the madness was soon too much and me, ross and max bolt without saying jack to the rest, it's the acid pact, when you're on it you just want to be around other people who are on it, everyone else is in the way man, it's that easy, off we go the great white bolting down the highway at unknowable speeds, unknowable destination and desire and fucked-up truancy, hmmmmmm…in a cemetery our backs to a headstone smoking cigarettes rolled out of ashtray butts cuz our money gone gone gone but trunk full of beer and lots of grass and late-night-ruminations acid already peaked and on the downslide now we're feeling contemplative and wise and talking earnestly in the cold -20 winter night not feeling the weather at all man too many chemicals in our bodies, too many ideas in our minds, too much sadness and wonder and good times galore and

the wind picked up and we continued cuz it's just weather and it don't mean a thing man, not a damn thing…

Tony Nesca was born in Torino, Italy in 1965 and moved to Canada at the age of three. He was raised in Winnipeg but relocated back to Italy several times until finally settling in Winnipeg in 1980. He taught himself how to play guitar and formed an original rock band playing the local bars for several years. At the age of twenty-seven he traded his guitar for a Commodore 64 and started writing seriously. He has published six chapbooks of stories and poems (which he used to sell straight out of his knapsack at local dives and bookstores), four novels, a novella, a book of poetry and has been an active contributor to the underground lit scene for ten years, being published in innumerable magazines both online and in print.

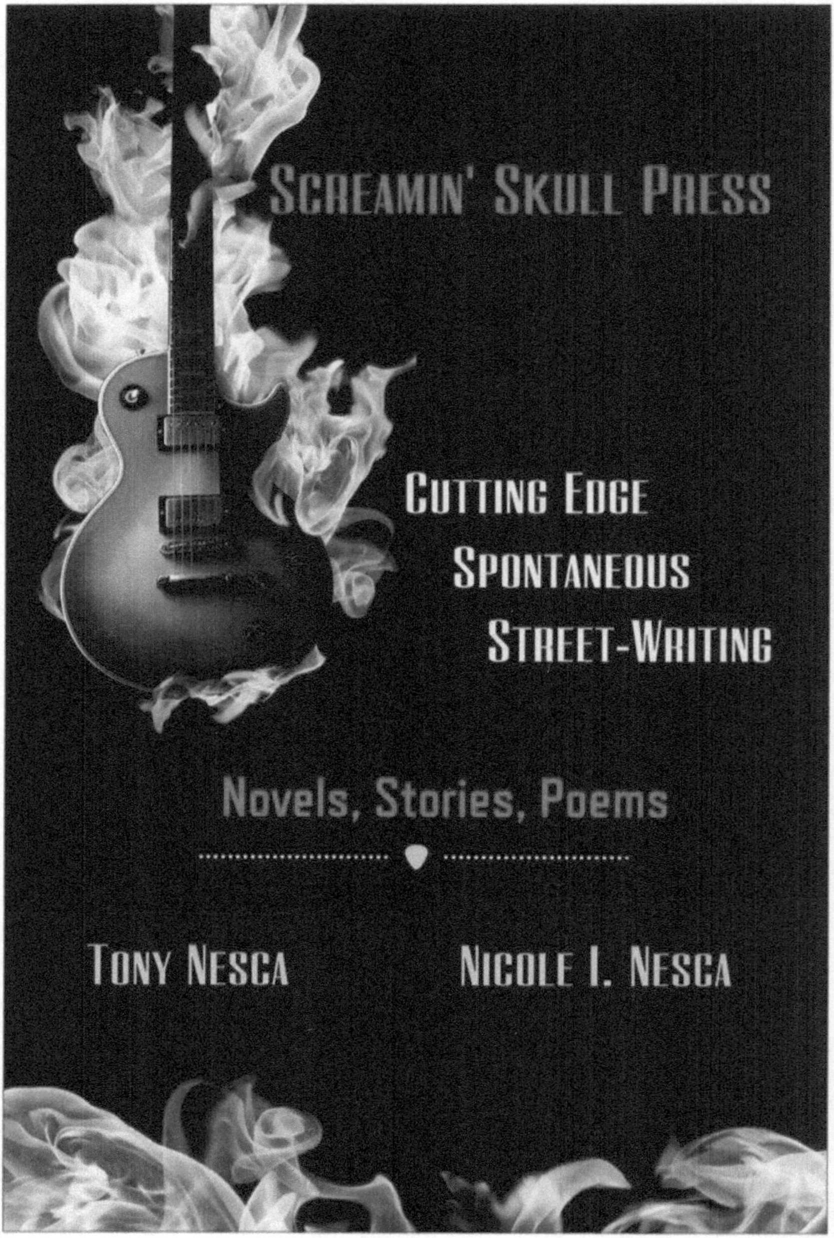
Screamin' Skull Press
Cutting Edge
Spontaneous
Street-Writing
Novels, Stories, Poems
Tony Nesca
Nicole I. Nesca

www.ingramcontent.com/pod-product-compliance
Lightning Source LLC
Chambersburg PA
CBHW031351170626
46807CB00002B/927
* 9 7 8 1 7 7 5 2 1 1 2 1 1 *